S

ALWAYS ALERT FOR DANGER IN
THE SOLAR SPHERE, SEARCHING
FOR NEW WORLDS AND BOLD ADVENTURE!

---

**Captain James Kirk**—The top man in Space Service—
Starship Command—he alone makes the decisions so
grave that they can affect the future course of civilization throughout the Universe.

**Lt. Uhura**—Unbelievably beautiful, she is the most pop-
ular member of the **Enterprise** crew and also one of
the most brilliant scan engineers around.

**Science Officer Spock**—Inheriting a precise, logical
thinking pattern from his father, a native of the planet
Vulcan, Mr. Spock maintains a dangerous Earth trait
. . . an intense curiosity about things of alien origin.

---

WITH A CREW OF 400 SKILLED
SPECIALISTS, THE MAMMOTH SPACE SHIP
**ENTERPRISE** BLASTS OFF FOR INTERGALACTIC
INTRIGUE IN THE UNEXPLORED REALMS OF OUTER SPACE

# STAR TREK 3

## ADAPTED BY JAMES BLISH

### BASED ON THE EXCITING NBC-TV SERIES CREATED BY GENE RODDENBERRY

BANTAM BOOKS · TORONTO · NEW YORK · LONDON

STAR TREK 3
*A Bantam Book / published April 1969*

*All rights reserved.*
*Copyright © 1969 by Bantam Books, Inc.*
*Copyright © 1969 by Paramount Pictures Corporation.*
*No part of this book may be reproduced in any form, by*
*mimeograph or any other means, without permission.*
*For information address: Bantam Books, Inc.*

*Published simultaneously in the United States and Canada*

*Bantam Books are published by Bantam Books, Inc., a subsidiary*
*of Grosset & Dunlap, Inc. Its trade-mark, consisting of the words*
*"Bantam Books" and the portrayal of a bantam, is registered in the*
*United States Patent Office and in other countries. Marca Registrada.*
*Bantam Books, Inc., 271 Madison Avenue, New York, N.Y. 10016.*

PRINTED IN THE UNITED STATES OF AMERICA

# CONTENTS

# PREFACE:

## Some Awards for *Star Trek*—and an Open Letter

Science-fiction fans hold an annual World Convention, which is held in a different city every year (though it has been outside the United States only once so far, in London in 1965). The most recent one, in Berkeley, Calif., was the twenty-sixth.

One of the many items on the program is the giving of achievement awards for the best s-f novel, novelette, short story and so on of the preceding year. These awards are statuettes called "Hugos," after the late Hugo Gernsback, who founded the first science-fiction magazine (*Amazing Stories*) in 1926.

In recent years, one of the categories has been "Best Dramatic Presentation," but there have seldom been many nominations for this category, and at at least one convention the decision was, "No award."

But since *Star Trek* came along, things have been different. At the 1967 convention in New York, the winner for Best Dramatic Presentation was Gene Roddenberry, not as originator and producer of *Star Trek* (though he was both), but as the author of the episode called "The Menagerie," which appeared during the show's first season.

And in 1968, *all four* of the nominees for Best Dramatic Presentation were from *Star Trek*. Three of those scripts are adapted in this collection; I have indicated them by asterisks.

What about the fourth? Well, the fourth was the actual

Hugo winner, "The City at the Edge of Forever," by Harlan Ellison. It is not in this collection for the simple reason that I had already put it in the preceding book, *STAR TREK TWO*. And judging by my mail, it was the heavy favorite there, too—which is a separate matter, since s-f fandom and *Star Trek* fandom do not seem to overlap very much, certainly by no more than 10 per cent.

The Hugo, by the way, was not Mr. Ellison's first award for that script; it was also voted the best single TV script of the year, regardless of category, by the television writers themselves. This award was given, however, not for the script as it ran on *Star Trek*, but for Mr. Ellison's original version, which had to be edited for the show—for one thing, it was too long. I mention this because readers of *STAR TREK TWO* may remember that in doing the adaptation of the script I tried to preserve what I thought were the best features of both versions. I feared that I might just have spoiled the whole thing in the process, but the readers' letters said not (and Mr. Ellison said not, too).

There is more that ought to be said about the fan mail, partly because it is, I think, interesting in itself, and partly in the hope that the facts might influence those sponsors and network officials who put too much faith in TV rating services. Beginning in 1951, I have written twenty-seven published novels and short-story collections (and including a volume of essays on science fiction). All of these books are still in print but one, and one of them was itself a Hugo winner. In addition, I've written many short stories and other kinds of material; the first one of these appeared early in 1940, and many have been anthologized—several of them repeatedly—in 58 different collections at last count. In 29 years my work has appeared in 18 different countries.

I note these figures not to brag—well, not entirely, anyhow—but as background for one astonishing fact: I have received more mail about my two previous *Star Trek* books than I have about *all my other work put together*.

I don't have to count the letters to establish this. All I have to do is look at the comparative thickness of two accordion file folders.

These letters have been arriving at an average rate of

two a day ever since January 1967. They make an astonishing collection. The writers range from children under 10, through college undergraduates (a large sub-group) to housewives. Not all the writers give their ages, of course, but enough of them do to make an adequate statistical sample, so I can say with fair confidence that the average age is 13. The *medium* age, however, is 15—that is, there are just as many writers over that age as there are under it.*

Most of them say that they have never read, or seen, any science fiction before *Star Trek,* or if they have, that they hadn't liked it. Some ask me to recommend other s-f books, or name some other books I have written. Still others announce a strong urge to write the stuff themselves, sometimes documented by accompanying manuscripts. In short, the evidence is strong that *Star Trek* has created an almost entirely new audience.

For over a year I tried to answer every one of these letters, however briefly, but the inroads this made on my creative writing time became a serious matter and I had to give it up, with regrets. (To give up answering the letters, that is!) However, there is one answer that I found myself making over and over which I would like to repeat here. That is the answer I gave to people who sent me *Star Trek* short stories, outlines, suggestions for scripts for the show, or even complete scripts:

"I have nothing to do with any aspect of the *Star Trek* show, including the selection of scripts. All I do is adapt some of the scripts into short stories. Furthermore, it is a firm rule of the producers that anyone even vaguely connected with the show who receives any sort of submission from anybody other than a recognized agent must return it unread, which is what I am doing in your case too. There are sound legal reasons for this which I'm sure you will understand.

"Furthermore, if you want to sell science fiction, your chances would be considerably greater if you tried to write a completely original story for one of the magazines, rather than basing your work on the characters and back-

---

*This difference shows that those over 15 are mostly young adults. The top *stated* age is 28.

ground of an already famous TV show. Originality is valued more highly in science fiction than in any other branch of literature. Hence, no matter what your affection for the *Star Trek* characters—which I share—you will in the long run be better off creating your own."

I have written those two paragraphs so many times that I could practically set them to music. Another I have written almost as often goes like this:

"I'm sorry, but I have no pictures from *Star Trek* to offer, nor can I send you a sample script—the scripts I have are the show's property, not mine. The place to write for further information is STAR TREK Enterprises, P.O. Box 38429, Hollywood, Calif. 90038. I myself have never been on the set, nor met any of the actors; and I have seen Mr. Roddenberry exactly three times, each time on a convention speakers' platform, along with about 800 other spectators."

Today I would like to add to this: Before you write, try a book called *The Making of Star Trek,* by Stephen E. Whitfield and Gene Roddenberry. (Ballantine Books, New York, #73004—414 pages, 95¢.) It almost surely contains the information you are looking for—and lots of pictures, too.

Finally: Thanks to all of you who suggested what scripts I might include in this book; I kept a tally, and abided by the voting. Thanks, too, to those who asked that I write an original *Star Trek* novel. Both the studio and Bantam agreed, somewhat to my surprise, that this was a good idea, so it's in the works.

So, to those of you who have written to me and haven't gotten an answer, I hope you will accept this as an apology and an explanation. At the least, I think it answers the most frequently asked questions.

JAMES BLISH

Brooklyn, N.Y.
1968

# THE TROUBLE WITH TRIBBLES*

## (David Gerrold)

Nobody seems to know where tribbles come from, though obviously they are comfortable in oxygen-bearing air at Earthlike temperatures and pressures. Newborn tribbles are about an inch long; the largest one ever seen, about sixteen inches.

A tribble looks a little like a cross between an angora cat and a beanbag. It has no arms or legs, no eyes, and in fact no face—only a mouth. It moves by rolling, by stretching and flexing like an inchworm, or by a peculiar throbbing which moves it along slowly but smoothly, rather like a snail. It does, however, have long fur, which comes in a variety of colors—beige, deep chocolate, gold, white, gold-green, auburn, cinnamon and dusky yellow.

Tribbles are harmless. Absolutely, totally, completely, categorically, inarguably, utterly, one hundred per cent harmless . . .

The *Enterprise* picked up a priority A-1 distress call from deep space station K-7 within a few moments after the big ship hove into sensor range. The station orbits Sherman's Planet, which is about three light years from the nearest Klingon outpost and hence well within the Klingon's sphere of influence—or the outpost was well within the Federation's sphere of influence, depending on how you looked at it.

---

*Hugo Award nominee

Both sides had claimed the planet. Although it was mostly barren, its position between the two political bodies was of considerable strategic importance. In the old days, one or the other would have grabbed it, and the other would have tried to jockey him off, at constant risk of war—a pastime the Klingons enjoyed.

These days, however, there was the Organian peace treaty to take into account. Under its terms, Sherman's Planet would belong to whichever side could prove it could develop the planet most effectively.

Under the circumstances, when a priority one distress call came from station K-7, the *Enterprise* could not be blamed for making for the station at Warp Six, with all hands at battle stations.

But when the ship arrived there was no target. K-7 rolled majestically and peacefully around Sherman's Planet, menaced—if that is the word—by nothing within sensor range but a one-man scout ship which floated nearby, obviously in parking orbit.

Baffled and irritated, Captain Kirk called the station's Commander Lurry, who refused any explanation except in person. He did so rather apologetically, but this did not placate Kirk in the least. He beamed over to the station with Spock, his First Officer—with orders to Sulu to keep the *Enterprise* at battle readiness.

There were two other men in Commander Lurry's office when Kirk and Spock arrived. Kirk paid no attention to them.

"Commander Lurry," he said, "you have sent out a priority one distress call. Please state the nature of your emergency."

"Uh, Captain, please allow me to explain. We in fact have no emergency, yet."

"Then you are in trouble," Kirk said grimly. "If there is no emergency, why did you order the call?"

One of the two unknowns said, "*I* ordered it, Captain."

"And who are you?"

"Captain Kirk, this is Nilz Baris," Lurry said. "He's out here from Earth to take charge of the development project for Sherman's Planet."

"And that gives you the authority to put a whole quadrant on defense alert?"

2

"Mr. Baris," the second unknown said stiffly, "is the Federation Undersecretary for Agricultural Affairs in this quadrant."

"A position with no military standing of which I am aware," Kirk said. "And who may *you* be, please?"

"This is my assistant, Arne Darvin," Baris said. "Now, Captain, I want all available security guards to . . ."

"I beg your pardon?" Kirk said. The way this trio had of answering questions for each other was not improving his temper, and thus far he had heard nothing even vaguely resembling an explanation.

"I will try to make myself clear," the Undersecretary said. "I want all available security guards. I want them posted around the warehouse. Surely that's simple enough."

"It's simple but it's far from clear. What warehouse?"

"The warehouse with the quadrotriticale," Darvin said, recapturing the ball. Lifting an attaché case to Lurry's desk, he extracted from it a small vial. From this he poured into his palm a few small seeds, which he handed to Baris, who in turn handed them to Kirk. The Captain inspected them briefly and then passed them on to Spock.

"Wheat," he said. "What about it?"

"Quadrotriticale is not wheat, Captain," Darvin said, with an audible sniff. "It is a newly developed form of trititicale."

"That leaves me as much in the dark as before."

"Trititicale is a high-yield per acre hybrid form of wheat and rye," Spock said quietly. "This appears to be a four-lobed rehybridization—a perennial, also, if I'm not mistaken. The root grain, triticale, traces its ancestry back to twentieth-century Canada."

"Uh, yes," Baris said, looking a little startled.

"And it is the only Earth grain that will grow on Sherman's Planet," Commander Lurry put in. "We have a warehouse of it here on the station. It's very important that the grain reach Sherman's Planet safely. Mr. Baris thinks that Klingon agents may try to sabotage it."

"Nothing could be more likely," the Undersecretary said. "That grain is going to be the way the Federation proves its claim to Sherman's Planet. Obviously the Klingons will do anything they can to keep it from getting there. It must be protected. Do you understand? It *must* be protected."

"So you issued a priority one distress call on behalf of a warehouse full of grain," Kirk said. "The only reason I don't arrest you on the spot is that I want the Federation to have Sherman's Planet as much as you do. Consider yourself lucky; misuse of the priority one channel is a Federation offense."

"I did not misuse . . ."

"Captain Kirk," Lurry interposed hurriedly, "couldn't you at least post a couple of guards? We do get a large number of ships passing through."

This of course was true. After a moment, Kirk said, "Mr. Spock, what do you think?"

"It would be a logical precaution, Captain."

"Very well." Kirk took out his communicator. "Kirk to *Enterprise* . . . Lieutenant Uhura, secure from general quarters. Next, beam over *two* security guards. Have them report to Commander Lurry."

"Yes, Captain."

"Also, authorize shore leave for all off-duty personnel. Kirk out."

"Only two?" Baris said, in something very like a fury. "Kirk, you're going to hear about this. I'm going to contact Starfleet Command."

"Do that," Kirk said, staring at the Undersecretary icily. "But before you put in the call, I suggest that you pin back your ears. It will save Starfleet Command the trouble of doing it for you."

The recreation area of K-7 was small, the shops little more than stalls surrounding a central mall formed by the intersection of a number of curving corridors. Space was at a premium.

As Kirk and Spock entered the area, a number of crew members from the *Enterprise* materialized on the mall, including Uhura and Sulu. Kirk moved toward them.

"I see you didn't waste any time getting over here," he said. "Mr. Sulu, we have a new specimen for your greenhouse. Mr. Spock?" The First Officer handed the grain over. "It's called . . ."

4

"Quadrotriticale!" the helmsman said eagerly. "I've read about it, but I've never seen any till now!"

"Come on, Sulu," Uhura said. "You can study it back aboard. Let's get in some shopping while we have the chance. Coming, Mr. Spock? Captain?"

"Well, for a few minutes, anyhow. But not for long; I suspect there are some hot messages shooting back and forth in subspace along about now."

The shop into which Uhura led them was vaguely cluttered and did not seem to specialize in anything in particular. Clearly it was one of those broker's establishments where spacemen on leave sold curios they had picked up on far planets, to help pay for their shore leaves—curios later resold to other spacemen for twice the price. This did not look like the best such shop Kirk had ever seen, but then, K-7 was not the best located of space stations, either.

There was nobody else in it at the moment but a tall, raffish-looking red-haired civilian, who had an immense quantity of merchandise spread out over the counter, and a carryall sack at his feet.

"No, absolutely not," the storekeeper was saying. "I've got enough Argilian flame gems to last me a lifetime. At the price I have to ask for them, hardly anybody on this junkyard can afford them."

"How sad for you, my friend," the peddler said. His voice was surprisingly melodious. "You won't see finer stones than mine anywhere. Ah well. Now surely you'll be wanting some Sirian glow water . . ."

"I use that," the storekeeper said in a deadly monotone, "to polish the flame gems."

The peddler sighed and swept most of his merchandise off the counter into his sack. Only one object was left—a green-gold ball of fluff.

"Ah, you are a most difficult man to reach. All I have left to offer you is tribbles. Surely, you will want . . ."

"Not at that price."

"Oooh," Uhura said. "What is it? Is it alive? May I hold him? He's adorable."

"What is it?" the peddler said, handing it over. "Why,

5

little darlin', it's a tribble. Only the sweetest little creature known to man—exceptin', of course, yourself."

The object in the lieutenant's hands throbbed gently. Kirk became aware of a low, pervasive sound, like a cross between the thrum of a kitten and the cooing of a dove. "Oh," Uhura said, "it's purring!"

"Ah, little lady, he's just sayin' that he likes you."

"Can I buy him?"

"That," the shopkeeper said, "is what we're trying to decide right now."

"My friend, ten credits apiece is a very reasonable price. You can see for yourself how much the lovely little lady here appreciates fine things. Others will, too."

"One credit," said the storekeeper.

Sulu put his grain on the counter and reached tentatively for the tribble. "He won't bite, will he?" the helmsman said.

"Sir!" the peddler said, making a great show of ignoring the storekeeper's offer. "There is a law against transporting harmful animals from one planet to another, as you as a starship officer must be fully aware. Besides, tribbles have no teeth."

"All right," the shopkeeper said. "Two credits."

The peddler took the tribble from Sulu and plopped it down on the counter again. "Nine," he said.

The shopkeeper eyed the animal dubiously. "Is he clean?"

"He's as clean as you are. I daresay a good deal cleaner."

"If you don't want him, I'll take him," Lt. Uhura said. "I think he's cute."

This set off another round of haggling. The two finally settled on six credits, whereupon the peddler began to produce more tribbles from his sack. Startlingly, no two were the same color or size.

"How much are you selling them for?" Uhura asked the shopkeeper.

"Ten credits. But for you . . ."

"Hey!" Sulu said suddenly. "He's eating my grain!" He swept up what remained. The tribble's purr got louder, and its non-face went slowly round and round, giving an absurd impression of bliss. The shopkeeper picked it up, but the peddler promptly took it from him.

"Sir," the peddler said. "That one happens to be my sample, which is mine to do with as I please. And I please to give it to the pretty little lady here."

"That's right," said the storekeeper. "Ruin the market."

"My friend," the peddler said, almost singing, "once the pretty little lady here starts to show this little precious around, you won't be able to keep up with 'em. Mark my words."

Lt. Uhura put the faceless ball of fur to her face, cooing alarmingly. Kirk did not know whether to be pleased or scared; Uhura had never shown the faintest sign of sentimentality before, but she seemed to be far gone in gooiness now. To be sure, the baggy little animals were attractive, but . . .

*Queep!*

No, that wasn't a tribble; it was his communicator.

"Kirk here."

"Captain, this is Scott. We have a stiff message in from Starfleet Command. I think you'd better deal with it; I don't think I'm authorized."

"All right, Scotty," Kirk told his communicator. "Record and hold. I'll be right over."

"Well and good. But, Captain, that's not all, sir. Our sensors have just picked up a Klingon battle cruiser. It's closing in rapidly on K-7. I've challenged it and gotten a routine acknowledgement; but . . ."

"Who's in command?" Spock said. Kirk had almost forgotten that he was still in the shop; but as usual, he had asked the crucial question. Kirk passed it on, with a grateful nod to his First Officer.

"Commander Koloth, sir. You'll remember him from our last encounter, Captain; a real, fourteen-karat son of a . . ."

"I get the message, Scotty. Hold on—and post battle stations. Lieutenant Uhura, pick up your pet; we're back on duty."

He had hardly finished speaking before the *Enterprise*'s transporters shimmered them all out of existence.

The message from Starfleet Command was, as usual, brief and pointed. It said: "It is not necessary to remind you of the importance to the Federation of Sherman's Planet. The key to our winning of this planet is the grain, quadrotriticale. The shipment of it must be protected. Effective immediately, you will render any aid and assistance which Undersecretary Baris may require. The safety of the grain—and the project—is your responsibility."

How complicated that was going to be was immediately made clear by the presence of the Klingon ship. It made no move to attack the station; that in fact would have been suicide, since every phaser on board the *Enterprise* was locked on the Klingon vessel (as Koloth, an able captain, would assume as a matter of course). Instead, Koloth stunned everyone by asking for shore leave for his men.

Under the Organian peace treaty, Commander Lurry had no choice but to grant the request. Starfleet, however, had inadvertently given Kirk a card to play, since the phrasing of the message had made the safety of the grain his responsibility. Hence he was able to order that only twelve Klingons be allowed shore leave at a time, and furthermore he beamed over one *Enterprise* security guard for every Klingon. That part of it, he thought, ought to please Baris, at least.

It did not please Baris. He did not want any Klingons on the station, period. He carried on about it quite a lot. In the end, however, it was clear that the Klingons had a right to be there, and nothing could be done about it.

Kirk stopped off at the recreation room for a cup of coffee and a breather. Scott, the engineer, was there reading a technical journal; that was his form of relaxation. Elsewhere, however, a knot of people were gathered around a table, including Spock, Dr. McCoy, Uhura and Ensign Freeman. Joining the group, Kirk found that on the table was Uhura's tribble and at least ten smaller ones; the crewmen were playing with them.

"How long have you had that thing, Lieutenant?" McCoy asked Uhura.

"Only since yesterday. This morning, I found that he— I mean *she* had had babies."

8

"I'd say you got a bargain." McCoy picked up one of the animals and examined it curiously. "Hmmm . . ."

"Lieutenant Uhura," Kirk said amusedly, "are you running a nursery?"

"I hadn't intended to—but the tribble had other plans."

Spock too was handling one of the creatures, stroking it absent-mindedly.

"You got it at the space station?" McCoy said.

"Yes, from the pilot of that one-man scout ship. Commander Lurry says his name is Cyrano Jones, of all things. He's a system locater, down on his luck."

"Most of them are," Kirk said. "Locating new systems on the margins of Klingon space is a synonym for locating trouble."

"A most curious creature, Captain," Spock said. "Its trilling would seem to have a tranquilizing effect on the human nervous system. Fortunately, I seem to be immune."

Watching his First Officer stroke the animal, Kirk raised an eyebrow, but offered no other comment.

"Lieutenant," McCoy said, "do you mind if I take one of these things down to the lab to find out what makes it tick?"

"It's all right with me, but if you're planning to dissect it, I don't want to know about it."

"Say, Lieutenant," Ensign Freeman said, "if you're giving them away, could I have one too?"

"Sure, why not? They seem to be old enough."

Freeman looked at Kirk. "I don't have any objections to pets on this ship," Kirk said. "Within reason. But if these tribbles want to stay on the *Enterprise,* they'd better be a little less prolific."

The tribbles, however, did not seem to get the message. Visiting sick bay the next day—another prolonged shouting match with Baris had given him a headache—Kirk found that McCoy had what seemed to be a boxful of the creatures.

"I thought Uhura gave you only one of those things, Bones. It looks more like you've got ten here."

"Average litter. I had eleven, but I dissected one. The

nearest thing I can figure out is that they're born pregnant."

"Is that possible?"

"No, but it would be a great timesaver, wouldn't it? I can tell you this much: almost fifty per cent of the creature's metabolism is geared to reproduction. Do you know what you get if you feed a tribble too much?"

Kirk's mind was not really on the subject. "A very fat tribble?"

"No. You get a whole bunch of hungry little tribbles. And if you think *that's* a boxful, you should see Uhura's. She's got about fifty, and she gave away five."

"Well, you'd better find homes for this batch before you've got fifty, too." Kirk swallowed the headache pill. "Are you going on shore leave, Bones?"

"Already been. Besides, this problem is more interesting. I understand Scotty went over with the last detachment; he'll see to it that there's no trouble. Unless, of course, the Klingons start it."

"I can't see why they'd want to do that. Koloth knows that if there is any, I'd promptly double the number of guards. If he's really after the grain, that's the last thing he'd want."

Nevertheless, after his next interview with Lurry, Kirk troubled to make a detour through the space station's bar. There were six Earthmen there, Scotty and Navigator Chekov among them. Five or six Klingons were at another table, but the two groups were studiously ignoring each other.

As Kirk joined his own men, Cyrano Jones entered the bar and also moved toward them. "Ah, friends," he said, "can I interest you in a tribble?"

He was holding one at Scott's shoulder. Scott turned toward him and found himself looking straight into the tribble's absence of a face. He shuddered.

"I've been pullin' the little beasties out of my engine room all morning!"

"Perhaps one of you other gentlemen—?" There was no response. With a fatalistic shrug, Cyrano went over to the Klingon table, approaching one whom Kirk recognized as Korax, one of Koloth's officers.

10

"Friend Klingon, may I offer you a charmin' little tribble . . ."

The tribble had other ideas. All its fur stood on end. It hitched itself up Cyrano's forearm with an angry spitting hiss.

"Stop that!" Cyrano said. "Apologies for his bad manners, sir. He's never done that before."

"I suggest," Korax said coldly, "that you remove yourself and that parasite as speedily as possible."

"It's only a friendly little . . ."

"Take it away!"

There was another hiss from the tribble. Korax slapped Cyrano's arm away, sending the tribble flying across the room to land among the Earthmen. Cyrano rushed to retrieve it; Scotty handed it to him without a word.

After looking from one group to the other, Cyrano, somewhat disconsolately, retreated to the bar, where the counterman was taking down a pitcher from a high shelf, and put his beast down on the counter.

"Sir! I feel sure that you would be willin' to engage in a little barter—one of my little tribbles in exchange for a spot of . . ."

The attendant turned, and upended the pitcher. Three tribbles fell out of it.

It was worse on shipboard. The corridors seemed to be crawling with the creatures. On the bridge, Kirk had to scoop three or four of them out of his chair before he could sit down. They were all over the consoles, on shelves, everywhere.

"Lieutenant, how did all of these tribbles get onto the bridge?"

"Through the ventilator ducts, I expect, Captain. They seem to be all over the ship."

"They certainly do. Mr. Spock, have a maintenance crew come up here to clean out this bridge. How many of them are there now, anyhow?"

"Assuming one creature—the one Lieutenant Uhura brought aboard—with an average litter of ten," the First Officer said, "every twelve hours. The third generation will total one thousand, three hundred thirty-one. The fourth generation will total fourteen thousand, six hundred and forty-one. The fifth generation will . . ."

"That's already enough. I want a thorough cleanup. They've got to go."

"All of them?" Lt. Uhura said protestingly. "Oh, Captain . . ."

"Every last one."

"A logical decision," Spock said. "Their breeding rate is beyond our control. They are consuming our supplies and returning nothing."

"Oh, come on now, Mr. Spock. I don't agree with you at all. They're giving us their love. Cyrano Jones says that a tribble is the only love money can buy."

"Lieutenant," Kirk said, "too much of anything—even love—is not necessarily a good thing. And in view of the fact that this all started with just one tribble, clearly the only safe number is none."

"And since feeding them is what makes them breed," Spock added, "one need only imagine what would happen if they got into the food processing machinery, or the food storage areas."

Kirk stared at the First Officer, thunderstruck. "Storage areas!" he said. "Great thundering fireballs! *Storage areas!* Lieutenant Uhura, contact Commander Lurry, and Nilz Baris. Have them meet us at the station mall. Mr. Spock, we're beaming over. Lieutenant, have Doctor McCoy join us in the transporter room—on the double!"

When the three materialized on the mall, half a dozen tribbles materialized with them. The mall did not need any more, however; it was inundated. The store where they had seen their very first tribble looked like a snow-bank of fur. The storekeeper, who had evidently just given up an attempt to sweep them out, was sitting in the midst of them with his head in his hands, close to tears.

Lurry and Baris came running to meet them—for once, without Darvin. "What's the matter?" Baris panted.

"Plenty—if what I think has happened, has happened. The warehouse, quick!"

Baris needed no further urging. They left at a dead run, kicking tribbles out of the way.

There were two guards before the warehouse door. "Is that door secure?" Kirk demanded.

"Yes, sir. Nothing could get in."

"Open it."

The guard produced a magnetic key. Nothing happened. "Don't understand it, sir. It seems to be . . ."

What it seemed to be will never be known, for at that moment the door slid open. There was a sort of silent explosion. Hundreds and hundreds and hundreds of tribbles came tumbling out, cascading down around them all, wriggling and seething and mewling and writhing and throbbing and trilling and purring . . .

They stood aghast as the mountain of fur grew. Spock recovered first. Scooping up a tribble, he examined it with clinical detachment. "It seems to be gorged," he observed.

"Gorged!" Baris gasped. "On my grain! Kirk! I'll hold you responsible! There must be thousands—hundreds of thousands!"

"One million, five hundred and sixty-one thousand, seven hundred and seventy-three," Spock said, "assuming, of course, that they got in here three days ago, and allowing for the maximum rate of grain consumption *and* the volume of the warehouse."

"What does the exact number matter?" Baris said despairingly. "The Klingons will get Sherman's Planet now!"

"I'm afraid," Kirk said slowly, "that you're right about that."

McCoy had been kneeling among the tribbles, examining them closely. At this point he looked up.

"Jim?"

"What is it, Bones?"

"Mr. Spock is wrong about these animals. They're not lethargic because they're gorged. They're dying."

"Dying! Are you sure?"

"I venture to say," McCoy replied with dignity, "that nobody on this station knows their metabolism better than I do. Yes, I am sure."

"All right," Kirk said with sudden energy. "Bones, take some of them back to your lab, and some of the grain, too. If they're dying, I want to know why. Then report back to me. I'm opening a formal hearing and investigation. Commander Lurry, I presume we can use your office. I'll want your assistant, and Captain Koloth—and Cyrano Jones, too."

"What good will that do?" Baris said. "The project is ruined—ruined!"

"Regulations require it," Kirk said. "And as for the project—well, that remains to be seen."

The scene in Lurry's office strongly resembled that moment in the classical detective novel when all the suspects are lined up and the shrewd sleuth eliminates all the obvious suspects and puts his finger on the butler. Lurry was seated behind his desk; nearby, in the visitor's chair, sat Cyrano Jones, stroking a tribble in his lap. Standing, with various degrees of uneasiness, interest or defiance, were Koloth, Korax, another Klingon aide, Spock, Baris, and McCoy, with Kirk facing them. And there were, of course, several security guards standing by. The Klingon captain spoke first:

"I had heard that you Earthers were sentimental about these parasites," he said, "but this is carrying things too far. I want an official apology from you, Kirk, addressed to the High Command of the Klingon Empire. You have restricted the shore leave of my men, harassed them with uniformed snoopers, and now summon us here like common criminals. If you wish to avoid a diplomatic crisis . . ."

"Don't do it, Kirk!" Baris burst in. "That'll give them the final wedge they need to claim Sherman's Planet!"

"Oh, as to *that* matter," Koloth said silkily, "it would seem that the outcome is already settled."

"One thing at a time," Kirk said. "Our present job is to find out who is responsible for the tribbles getting into the quadrotriticale. The Klingons have an obvious motive. On the other hand, it was Cyrano Jones who brought them here, apparently with purely commercial intent. There's no obvious connection."

"Beggin' your pardon, Captain," Cyrano said, "but a certain amount of the blame might be lyin' in sheer ignorance of the little creatures. If you keep their diet down below a certain intake per day, why sure and they don't breed at all. That's how I control mine."

Kirk stared at him. "Why didn't you tell us that before?"

"Nobody asked me. Besides, Captain, any man's com-

14

mon sense should tell him that it's bad for little animals to be overfeedin' 'em."

"Let that pass for the moment. We also need to find out what killed the tribbles. Was the grain poisoned—and if so, who poisoned it?"

He looked fixedly at Koloth, but the Klingon only smiled. "I had no access to it, obviously," he said. "Your guards were watching me every instant. However, Captain, before we go on—would you mind very much having that thing taken out of here?"

He pointed at the tribble in Cyrano's lap. Kirk hesitated a moment, but he could in fact sympathize; he had himself seen enough tribbles to last him a lifetime. He gestured to a guard, who lifted the creature gingerly and moved toward the door.

At the same moment, the door opened and Darvin entered belatedly. The tribble fluffed itself up and spat.

Kirk stared at it a moment in disbelief. Then, taking it from the crewman, he crossed over to Korax and held it out; it spat again. It spat at the third Klingon, too, and at Koloth. However it purred for everyone else, even including Baris—oh well, Kirk thought, there's no accounting for some people's tastes—and it went into a positive ecstasy over Spock, to the First Officer's rigidly controlled distaste. Then back to Darvin. *Hisssss!*

"Bones!" Kirk barked. "Check this man!"

McCoy was already at Darvin's side, tricorder out. He ran it over the man twice.

"It figures, Jim," he said. "Heartbeat all wrong, body temperature—well, never mind the details. He's a Klingon, all right."

The security men closed on Darvin. "Well, well," Kirk said. "What do you think Starfleet Command will have to say about this, Mr. Baris? Bones, what did you find out about the grain?"

"Oh. It wasn't poisoned. It was infected."

"Infected," Baris repeated in a dull voice. He seemed past reacting to any further shock.

"Yes. It had been sprayed with a virus which practices metabolic mimicry. You see, the molecules of the nutriments the body takes in fit into the molecules of the body itself like a key into a lock. This virus mimics the key—

but it isn't a nutriment itself. It blocks the lock so the proper nutriments can't get in. A highly oversimplified explanation, but good enough for the purpose."

"Do I mean you to imply," Kirk said, "that the tribbles starved to death? A whole warehouse full of grain, and they starved in the midst of it?"

"That's essentially it," McCoy agreed.

"And would this have happened to any *men* who ate the grain?"

"It would happen to any warm-blooded creature. The virus is very catholic in its tastes—like rabies."

"I observe another possible consequence," Spock said. "Dr. McCoy, could the virus be killed without harming the grain?"

"I think so."

"In that case," Spock said, "Mr. Darvin's attempt at mass murder has done us all a favor, and so have Mr. Jones' tribbles."

"I don't follow you, Mr. Spock," Kirk said.

"A simple logical chain, Captain. The virus without doubt prevented the tribbles from completely gutting the warehouse; fully half the grain must be left. On the other hand, the tribbles enabled us to find that the grain was infected without the loss of a single human life."

"I don't think the Federation courts will count that much in Mr. Darvin's favor, Mr. Spock, but it's a gain for us, I agree. Guards, take him out. Now, Captain Koloth, about that apology—you have six hours to get your ship out of Federation territory."

Koloth left, stiffly and silently. The tribble hissed after him.

"I hate to say this," Kirk said, "but you almost have to love tribbles just for the enemies they make. Now, Mr. Jones. Do you know what the penalty is for transporting an animal that is proven dangerous to human life? It is twenty years."

"Ah, now, Captain Kirk," Cyrano said, almost in tears. "Surely we can come to some form of mutual understanding? After all, as Mr. Spock points out, my little tribbles did tip you off to the infection in the grain—and they proved a most useful Geiger counter for detecting the Klingon agent."

16

"Granted," Kirk said gravely. "So if there's one task you'll undertake, I won't press charges, and when you're through with it, Commander Lurry will return your scout ship to you. If you'll remove every tribble from this space station . . ."

Cyrano gasped. "Remove every tribble? Captain, that'll take years!"

"Seventeen point nine years," Spock said, "to be exact."

"Think of it as job security," Kirk suggested.

"It's either this—or charges? Ah, Captain, you're a hard man—but I'll do it."

There was not a single tribble about the *Enterprise* when the party returned. It proved rather difficult to find out how this miracle had been brought about, but Scotty finally admitted to it.

"But how did you do it?"

"Oh, I just had the cleanup detail pile them all into the transporter."

"But—Scotty, you didn't just transport them out into space, did you?"

The engineer looked offended. "Sir, I'm a kindhearted man. I gave them a good home, sir."

"Where? Spit it out, man!"

"I gave them to the Klingons, sir. Just before they went into warp, I transported the whole kit and kaboodle into their engine room. And I trust, sir, that all their tribbles will be big ones."

# THE LAST GUNFIGHT

## (Lee Cronin)

As the *Enterprise* approached the Melkotian system, her sensors picked up an orbiting buoy which Captain Kirk thought it best to investigate. He had orders to contact the Melkotians "at all costs"—no explanation, just "at all costs"—but he was a peaceable man, and it was his experience that peoples who posted buoys around their planetary domains had a tendency to shoot if such markers were passed without protocol.

The buoy's comments were not encouraging. It said: "Aliens. You have encroached on the space of the Melkot. You will turn back immediately. This is the only warning you will receive."

Kirk's unease at the content of this message was almost eclipsed by his surprise in receiving it in English. The uneasiness returned full force when he promptly discovered that Spock had heard it in Vulcan, Chekov in Russian, and Uhura in Swahili.

"True telepaths," Spock summed up succinctly, "can be most formidable."

This was inarguable, as was the fact that absolutely nothing was known about the Melkotians but the fact of their existence. The orders were also inarguable. Kirk broadcast a message of peaceful intent, and getting no answer—not that he had expected any—proceeded, wondering what in the Universe a race of true telepaths could be afraid of.

When the ship was in range, Kirk beamed down to the

planet, accompanied by Spock, McCoy, Scott and Chekov. The spot on which they materialized was a sort of limbo—a place of twisting fog, unidentifiable shapes, feelings, colors. Spock's tricorder refused to yield any further information; it was as though they were in some sort of dead spot where no energy could flow, or at least none could enter. To Kirk it felt rather more like the eye of a hurricane.

Then the Melkotian materialized—or partially materialized, almost like an image projected against the fog. He was essentially humanoid: a tall, thin, robed figure, with cold pale features, a high forehead, and piercing eyes that seemed to be utterly without feeling.

"Our warning was plain," he said in his illusion of many languages. His lips did not move. "You have disregarded it. You, Captain Kirk, ordered this disobedience. Therefore from you we shall draw the pattern of your death."

"Death!" Kirk said. "For trespassing? Do you call yourselves civilized?"

"You are Outside," the figure said. "You are Disease. We do not argue with malignant organisms; we destroy them. It is done."

The figure winked out. "Talk about your drumhead court martials," Scott said.

No one heard him, for the limbo had winked out at the same time. Instead, the five men appeared to be standing in a desert, in bright, hot sunlight. As they stared, a wooden building popped into existence; then another, and another. None of them were more than two storeys high, generally with porches at the second storey. One of them bore a sign reading, "Saloon," another, "Tombstone Hotel." Within seconds they were surrounded by a town.

"Spock," Kirk said quietly. "Evaluation."

"American frontier, circa 1880," Spock said.

"And what's this?" Chekov said, holding out a gun. It was not a phaser. A quick check showed that none of them any longer had a phaser, or a communicator; only these pieces of ironware, slung low around their hips from belts loaded with what appeared to be ammunition. Their uniforms, however, had not changed.

19

"That," Kirk said, "is a Colt .45—perfect for the period. My ancestors came from a background like this."

"Perfect, but dangerous, Captain," Spock said. "I suggest we dispose of them."

"Certainly not, Mr. Spock. Whatever the Melkotians plan for us, it's not likely to be pleasant. And at close range, these things are as deadly as phasers. We may have to use them as such."

"Jim, that shack over there calls itself Tombstone Epitaph," McCoy said. "Sounds like a newspaper. And there's a bulletin board on it. Let's see if we can pick up a little more information."

The bulletin board carried a copy of the day's paper. It was dated Tombstone, Arizona, October 26, 1881.

"Back in time, Mr. Spock?" Kirk said.

"And an instantaneous space crossing as well, Captain?" Spock said. "I don't care to entertain the notion of so many physical laws being violated at the same time. The energy expenditure alone would be colossal—far beyond anything we've ever detected on Melkot. I suspect we are exactly where we were before."

"Then what's the purpose of this—this setup?"

"As I understand it, Captain," Spock said gently, "the purpose is an execution."

"We can always depend on you for a note of cheer," McCoy said.

There was something about the date that nagged at Kirk's mind. As he was trying to place it, however, an unshaven man came around a corner, saw the five men, and stared. Then he said:

"Well, I'll be jiggered! Ike! Frank, Billy, Tom!" He came closer. "I was afraid you weren't going to make it."

"I beg your pardon?" Kirk said.

"But I knew you wouldn't let 'em scare you away. They're a lot of hot air, if you ask me. But now they'll have to fight, after the way they've shot off their mouths."

"Look here," Kirk said. "Obviously you think you know us. But we don't know you. We've never seen you before."

The unshaven man winked solemnly. "I getcha. I ain't seen you today, neither. That's what I like about you, Ike, you always see the funny side. And nobody can say Johnny Behan doesn't have a sense of humor."

"I'm a barrel of laughs," Kirk said. "But look, Mr. Behan . . ."

"Just one thing," Behan said. "I wouldn't take them too lightly if I was you. They may shoot wild, but they're gonna have to shoot."

As if alarmed by what he himself had said, Behan shot a glance over his shoulder and scuttled off. At the same instant, Kirk grasped the memory he had been struggling for.

"The Earps!" he said. Spock looked baffled; so did the others.

"He called me Ike," Kirk said. "And he called you Frank, and Bones, Tom, and Chekov, Billy. That's Ike Clanton, Frank and Tom McClowery, Billy Claiborne and Billy Clanton."

"Captain," Spock said, "I know something about this segment of Earth history, but those names mean nothing to me."

"Me either," McCoy said.

"All right. Try Wyatt Earp. Morgan Earp. Virgil Earp. Doc Holliday." There was no reaction. "It goes like this. In the late nineteenth century, in Arizona, two factions fought it out for control of the town of Tombstone. The Earps were the town marshals. The Clantons were lined up with Billy Behan, the County Sheriff. And on October 26, they had it out."

"And?" Chekov said.

"The Clantons lost, Mr. Chekov."

There was silence. At last Spock said, "This is certainly a most fanciful method of execution. But what did they mean by . . ."

A woman's scream cut through the still, hot air. From the direction of the saloon came a roar of men's voices and the unmistakable sounds of a brawl. Then a man stumbled backwards out of the swinging doors and fell down the steps into the street. Another man came after him like a flash.

As the first man picked himself up out of the dust, he reached quickly for his holster. He was way too late. His

21

pursuer's gun went off with an astonishingly loud noise, like a thunderclap, and his twisted body was hurled back almost to Kirk's feet. The second man turned and went back through the swinging doors without another glance.

McCoy knelt beside the body and took its pulse. "Cold-blooded murder," he said angrily.

"I believe the phrase," Spock said, "is 'frontier justice.' "

"I can't believe it's real," Chekov said. "It's all just some sort of Melkotian illusion."

"Is the man dead, Bones?"

"Very dead, Jim."

"Well," Kirk said grimly, "that seems to be at least one thing that's real here."

From the saloon came a burst of music—a piano, recognizable in any era—and a shout of laughter. The five from the *Enterprise* looked down at the lonely dead man, and then, in almost a nightmare of compulsion, at the saloon.

"I think," Kirk said, "we'd better find out what's happening."

"Go in *there*?" Chekov said.

"Has anybody a better idea?"

There was a bartender, a pretty and very young waitress, and about a dozen customers; most of the latter were clustered around the killer of a moment before, who sat at a table. He rose slowly as the five came through the doors.

"Ike, Tom," the bartender said. He seemed both pleased and scared to see them. Here, at least, the Clantons had some sort of friend. "Hiya, boys. Didn't think we'd see you again."

The waitress turned. "Billy!" she cried with delight, and flinging herself on the astonished and delighted Chekov, kissed him thoroughly. "Billy baby, I knew they couldn't keep you out of town."

"I didn't have much choice," Chekov said.

The girl led them toward a table a good distance away from that of the killer. "But maybe you shouldn't have," she said.

"And passed up the chance to see you? Don't be silly."

"But it's takin' crazy chances, with Morgan right in the same room."

22

Kirk, who had sat down, rose slowly again to get a closer look at the first of the men at whose hands they had been condemned to die. "Of course," he said. "The gentleman who kills on sight. Morgan Earp."

Earp did not move, but he watched Kirk with stony intentness.

"Captain," Spock said, *sotto voce,* "since we have seen that death is the one reality in this situation, I seriously advise that you reseat yourself without moving a muscle of either hand. Otherwise you will find yourself involved in something called 'the fast draw,' if I remember correctly. The results would be unfortunate."

Kirk sat down. As he did so, the bartender called, "You boys want your usual?"

"Absolutely," Scotty said enthusiastically. "Half a liter of Scotch."

"You know we ain't got nothin' but bourbon. 'Less you want gin."

"I don't think we've got the time for a party," Kirk said. He looked at Chekov, in whose lap the girl was now sitting. "Of any kind."

"What can I do, Captain? You know we're always supposed to maintain good relations with the natives."

"That's all right," the girl said, getting up. "I know you boys have got some palaverin' to do. Billy Claiborne, you be careful." She hurried away.

"Mr. Spock," Kirk said, "except for these handguns we're wearing, we haven't changed. Not even our clothing. Yet these people see us as the Clantons."

"I don't find that such a bad thing, Captain," Chekov said, his eyes still following the waitress.

"The day is still young, Ensign," Spock said.

"Now then, what have we got? We're in Tombstone on the day of the fight at the OK Corral, and we're the Clanton gang. Morgan Earp there will tell his brothers we're here."

"And history will follow its course," Spock said.

"It will not," Kirk said angrily. "I have no intention of letting a bunch of half-savage primitives kill us."

"May I ask, Captain, how you plan to prevent it?"

Without replying directly, Kirk got up and went over to the bar. "You, Mr. Bartender. You claim to know us."

"Ain't makin' no big claims about it to nobody," the bartender said. "Jest so happens."

"Well, you're wrong. You think I'm Ike Clanton. I'm not. I'm James T. Kirk, Captain of the Starship *Enterprise*. And these men are some of my officers. We're not really here at all; in fact, we haven't been born yet."

There was a roar of laughter from the onlookers, and somebody said, "Don't you jest bet he wishes he hadn't been."

Kirk whirled to the nearest man. "Here, you. Feel the material of my shirt." The man snickered, but complied. "Doesn't it feel any different from yours?"

"Reckon it does," the cowboy said. "A mite cleaner, I'd jedge."

"Have you ever seen men wearing clothes like these before?"

The cowboy thought a moment. Then he said earnestly, "Sure. On the Clantons."

There was another outburst of laughter and thigh-slapping.

"Looka here, now," the cowboy said. "You was always a great one for jokin', Ike. But I know you. Ed here," indicating the barkeeper, "knows you. That Sylvia, she sure knows Billy Claiborne. Now, if'n you want to pertend you're somebody else, that's your business. Only, if you've turned yellow, what'd you come back to town for at all?"

Kirk frowned and tried to think, twirling his gun absently. The cowboy turned pale and backed away a step. Realizing belatedly what he had done, Kirk returned the gun to its holster and swung back to the barkeeper.

"Ed . . ."

"It's okay with me, Ike," Ed said placatingly. "Anything you say. It don't make no difference who I think you are. Your problem is—who does Wyatt Earp think you are?"

Hopelessly, Kirk returned to the table. His men looked at him strangely. What was the matter with *them,* now?

"Well, scratch that," he said, sitting down. "I can't get through to them."

"Captain."

"Yes, Mr. Spock."

"We know that the Melkotians are true telepaths. And

24

the Melkot said that it was from you that he would 'draw the pattern' of our deaths."

"Are you suggesting that because I'm familiar with this part of American history . . . ?"

"He looked into your mind, and selected what he considered to be the best time and place for our punishment. Yes, Captain. While you were pacing back and forth up there at the bar, I was recalling certain tapes in the computers. All unconsciously, you are adopting the true gunfighter's slouch. And a moment ago, you were handling the weapon like an expert."

"Some inherited characteristic?" McCoy said. "Ridiculous. Acquired characteristics can't be inherited."

"I know that, Dr. McCoy," Spock said stiffly. "The suggestion was yours, not mine. On the other hand, the possibility of ancestral memories—archetypes drawn from the collective unconscious, if such a thing exists—has never been disproved. And you observed the Captain's behavior yourself. As a further test, would you care to draw your own gun and twirl it, then return it smoothly to its holster, as the Captain did?"

"I wouldn't dare," McCoy admitted. "I'd be better off with a club."

"Let me make sure I understand this," Kirk said. "Do you further suggest that the Melkot is counting on me to act completely like one of these frontiersmen? To respond instinctively to the challenge of the Earps, and so bring about our—end?"

"Not instinctively, Captain, but certainly unconsciously. It's a possibility you must be on guard against."

"I'll bear it in mind. Now, has anybody any other suggestions for breaking this pattern?"

"Why don't we just get out of town, Captain?" Chekov said.

"There is no such place as 'out of town,'" Spock said. "Bear in mind, Ensign Chekov, that we are actually on the planet of the Melkots. Were we to leave this area, they would have no more difficulty in returning us to it than they did in putting us in it in the first place."

"Logic again," McCoy said. "Why don't you forget logic for a while and try to think of something that *would* work? If we only had a phaser—or better yet, a communi-

25

cator! It'd be a pleasure to see the faces of those Earps as we were beamed back to the ship exactly thirty seconds before the big blow-down, or whatever it's called."

"Bones, you have a point," Kirk said. "Mr. Spock, when we were thrown back in time from the City on the edge of Forever, you managed to construct a functioning computer out of your tricorder. And you've got a tricorder here."

"But we were thrown back then to the Chicago of the 1930's," the First Officer said. "In those days, the technology was just barely up to supplying me with the necessary parts and power. Here we have no gem stones to convert to tuning crystals, no metals to work, not even a source of electricity."

"He's quite right there, Captain," Scott said. "I couldn't turn the trick myself, under these conditions."

"Then," Kirk said, "it would appear that we're limited to contemporary solutions."

"Maybe not," McCoy said thoughtfully. "We have gunpowder in these shells. And surely there are drugs of some kind in town. One of the Earp crowd is called 'Doc' . . . "

"He was a dentist," Kirk said.

"Nevertheless, he must have drugs, herbs of some kind. Cotton wadding. A mortar and pestle. Alcohol—we can use whisky for that if we have to."

"What do you have in mind?" Kirk said.

"What would happen if we turned up at the OK Corral with no guns at all—just slingshots—*and tranquilizing darts?*"

Slowly, Kirk began to grin. "A fine notion. What's the first step, Bones?"

"I'll go and see Doc Holliday."

"But he's one of the opposition. We'd better all go."

"Absolutely not," McCoy said. "That would start shooting for sure. I'll go by myself, and see what I can talk him out of, as one medical man to another. And the rest of you, if I may so suggest, had better drop out of sight until I get back."

"All right, Bones," Kirk said slowly. "But watch yourself."

"I'll do that," McCoy said. "It's myself I'm fondest of in all the world."

Doc Holliday's office, as it turned out, was in a barber-shop. As McCoy entered, he had a patient in the chair. Doc Holliday was pulling; the patient was kicking and hollering. McCoy stared with fascination over Holliday's shoulder.

Holliday had evidently never heard of white coats. He was wearing a black frock coat, tight pants, a flat hat, and a string tie—a more elaborate version of the outfit McCoy had seen on Morgan Earp.

After a moment of watching the dentist sweat, McCoy said, "Impacted, I gather."

Holliday grunted abstractedly. Then apparently recognizing the voice, he leapt back, clearing his coat tail from his gun. He glared at McCoy.

"You want it now, McClowery?"

"Actually, the family name is McCoy."

"Look Doc," the patient said, looking up impatiently. "Are you going to pull it now, or—" Then he, too, recognized McCoy and turned white as milk. "Boys, please, no shootin'! Doc, put away your gun."

He tried to get out of the chair; Holliday slammed him back into it. "Sit!" the dentist said. "I ain't been through all that for nothin'. As fer you, McClowery, if you're goin' t'backshoot a medical man in the performance of his duties . . ."

"Not at all. I'm interested in medical matters myself. Mind if I take a look?" McCoy pried open the patient's mouth and peered in. "Hmm, that tooth is in sad shape, all right. What do you use for anesthetic, Preliform D? No, of course you don't have that yet. Chloroform? Is it possible you actually use chloroform? If so, why isn't the patient asleep?"

"What do you know about it, McClowery?"

"I've pulled a few teeth myself."

"I use whisky," Holliday said. "I never heard of chloroform."

"Tricky stuff, alcohol. You think the patient's too drunk to know his own name, and then there's a little pain, and bang! He's cold sober. Especially with a badly impacted tooth like that. Probably needs some root canal work, too."

"Whisky's all I got," Holliday said, a little sullenly.

"Well, actually, you don't need an anesthetic at all. Simple matter of pressure. A Vulcan friend of mine showed it to me. If you don't mind—" he took the crude pliers from Holliday, examined them, and shrugged. "Well, they'll have to do."

"Now look, McClowery . . ."

"No, you look, Doctor." McCoy thrust a finger into the patient's mouth. "There's a pressure point above the superior mandible—right here. Press it—hard, mind you—then you . . ."

He reached in with the pliers, closed, tugged. In a moment he was holding the tooth before Holliday's astonished face.

"Hey!" said the patient. "What happened? Did you—it's gone! It's gone—and I didn't feel a thing!"

"Nothing?" Holliday said incredulously.

"Not a thing."

"Where'd you learn that trick, McClowery?"

"You'd never believe me if I told you. Doctor, you're from the South, aren't you?"

"Georgia."

"Is that a fact! I'm from Atlanta myself."

"Is that so? I never knew that," Holliday said. "Now that's a cryin' shame, me havin' to kill another Georgia man, with this place crawlin' with Yankees and all."

"Actually, I could do you a favor, if I had time. You're not well, Doctor. Those eyes—that pallor—by George, I've never seen a case before, but I do believe you have tuberculosis. If I could run a quick physical . . ."

With a roar of rage, Holliday slammed his six-shooter on the table top. The patient sprang from the barber's chair and ran.

"One more peep out of you," Holliday said, "and you won't even hold water!"

"Why? What are you so mad about?"

"I may have bad lungs, but I've got a good aim!"

"Doctor," McCoy said, "if I had my kit here, I could clear those lungs up with one simple injection. One shot, twelve hours of rest, and the disease would be gone. Without the kit, it'll have to take more time."

"Time is just what you're short on," Holliday said.

"You seem like a halfway decent sort, though. Why don't you play it smart and come in with us?"

"What—double-cross Kirk?"

"No, just the Clantons."

"Can't do it," McCoy said. "But if you don't mind our parting friends for the moment, I'd like to borrow a few drugs."

Holliday gestured expansively. "A favor for a favor. Just don't expect me to shoot wild at five o'clock tonight."

It was just that casually that McCoy learned the hour of their death.

As he emerged into the street, the sunlight blinded him for a moment. Then he became aware that Sylvia was crossing the street near him, her eyes averted. He was puzzled at the apparent cut—after all, she had seemed friendly enough to the Clantons in the saloon—and then realized that there were three other men on his side of the street, lounging outside the Marshal's office. All three were wearing the same kind of outfit as Holliday, and since one of them was Morgan, it did not take much guessing to figure out that the other two must be Virgil and Wyatt Earp.

McCoy stepped back into the doorway of the barbershop. At the same time, Morgan grinned, nudged one of his brothers, and stepped out to cut Sylvia off.

"What's the matter, honey?" he said, taking her elbow.

Sylvia tugged at her arm. "Let me go!"

"I'm just letting you get a jump on things. After tonight, there ain't goin' to be any Billy Claiborne."

Both the watching brothers tensed suddenly, their grins fading. McCoy followed the direction of their stares. To his horror, he saw Chekov coming down the middle of the street, jaw set, face flushed.

Morgan saw him too. He gently thrust the girl to one side, still holding her with his left hand. "Well," he said. "Here he is—the baby who walks like a man."

"Take your hands off her, you . . ."

Morgan abruptly thrust Sylvia away. Chekov went for his gun, but there was only one shot; Chekov's gun didn't even clear his holster. With a look of infinite surprise, he clawed at the growing red stain on the front of his tunic, and then pitched forward on his face.

McCoy was already running, and as he hit the dirt, he saw Kirk and Spock rounding a corner at top speed. Morgan Earp stepped back a few paces, contemptuously. McCoy fell to his knees beside Chekov, just in time to feel the last feeble thrill of life flutter out.

He looked up at Kirk. Scotty was there too; God knew where he had arrived from.

"Bones?" Kirk whispered, his face gray.

"I can't do a thing, Jim."

Kirk looked slowly toward the smiling Earps. Fury began to take possession of his face. McCoy heard the grating noise of the barbershop door opening; evidently Doc Holliday was coming out to join his confreres.

"Well, Ike?" Wyatt Earp said softly. "Want to finish it now?"

Kirk took a step forward, his hand dropping toward his gunbutt. Spock and Scott grabbed him, almost simultaneously. "Let me go," Kirk said, in a low, grinding voice.

"Yeah, let him go," Morgan said. "Let's see how much stomach he's got."

"Control yourself, Captain," Spock said.

McCoy rose slowly, keeping his own hand near his gun, though it felt heavily strange and useless on his hip; it occurred to him that the thing was at least three times as heavy as a phaser. "Easy, Jim," he said. "You wouldn't have a chance. None of us would."

"They murdered that boy! You think I'm going to . . ."

"You've got to," Scott said intensely. "You lose *your* head and where would the rest of us be? Not just the laddie, but . . ."

"More data," Spock said. "Jim, listen to me. We need more data."

"Smart, Clanton," Wyatt said. "Get as much living in as you can."

Slowly, slowly, Kirk allowed himself to be turned away. His face was terrible with grief.

In a back room of the saloon, Spock fitted nail points to darts; McCoy dipped the points into a mortar which contained a tacky brown elixir—his improvised tranquilizing drug. Five even more improvised slingshots lay to hand, as did an almost denuded feather duster—supplied by Sylvia—from which Spock had fletched the darts.

"I can only hope these will fly true," Spock said. "A small hand-driven wind tunnel would help, but we have no time to build one."

"Somehow I can't seem to care," Kirk said. "Sometimes the past won't let go. It cuts too deep. Hasn't that ever happened to you?"

"I understand the feeling, Captain."

" 'I understand the feeling,' " McCoy mimicked angrily. "Chekov is dead and you talk about what another man feels. What do *you* feel?"

"My feelings are not a subject for discussion."

"There aren't any to discuss," McCoy said disgustedly.

"Can that be true?" Kirk said. "Chekov is dead. I say it now, yet I can hardly believe it. You knew him as long as I did, you worked with him as closely. That deserves its memorial."

"Spock will have no truck with grief," McCoy said. "It's human."

"I did not mean any disrespect to your grief," Spock said from behind his mask. "I, too, miss Ensign Chekov."

There was silence for a moment. Dully, Kirk realized that they had been unfair to the First Officer. No matter how often we run into the problem, he thought, we'll never get used to Spock's hidden emotional life.

Upstairs, a grandfather clock struck four. Time was running out.

"Captain, I've been thinking," Spock said. "I know nothing about the history of the famous gun battle we seem about to be engaged in. Was the entire Clanton gang involved?"

"Yes."

"Were there any survivors?"

"Let me think—yes. Billy Claiborne—*Billy Claiborne!*"

"Thus we are involved in a double paradox. The real Billy Claiborne was in the battle. 'Our' Billy Claiborne will not be. The real Billy Claiborne survived the fight. 'Ours' is already dead. History has already been changed."

"And maybe we can change it again," Kirk said with

31

dawning hope. "Bones, how long will that tranquilizer goo of yours need to take effect?"

"No more than three or four seconds, I think. But of course it hasn't been tested. No experimental animals."

"Try it on me," Scotty suggested. "I have an animal nature."

"Well—a dilute solution, maybe. Okay. Roll up your sleeve."

"Captain," Spock said, "may I propose that this is also an opportunity to see how the darts fly? We can put Dr. McCoy's dilute solution on one."

"Too dangerous. Slingshots can kill at short range. Remember David and Goliath."

"Vaguely. But I do not propose to use a sling—only to throw the dart by hand."

Scott ambled across the room to a bureau, on which he leaned like a man leaning on a bar, imaginary glass in hand, his hip thrust out. "How's this?"

"A prime target." Spock threw the dart, gently, underhand. It lodged fair and square in Scott's left buttock. He said, "Oof," but held the pose. They watched him intently.

Nothing happened. After five long minutes, McCoy went over to him and withdrew the dart. "It penetrated the muscle," he said. "It should have worked by now. Feel anything, Scotty?"

"Nothing at all."

"No sweating? No dizziness? No palpitations?"

"I never felt better in my life."

McCoy's face fell. "I don't understand it," he said. "Full strength, that stuff should knock out a charging elephant."

"Fascinating," Spock said.

"Fascinating!" Kirk exploded. "Mr. Spock, don't you realize that this is our death warrant? There isn't time to devise anything else!"

"It is nevertheless fascinating," Spock said slowly. "First a violation of physics, then a violation of history—now a violation of human physiology. These three violations cannot be coincidence. They must contain some common element—some degree of logical consistency."

32

"Well, let's see if we can think it through," Kirk said. "But there's one last chance. We may be able to violate history again. Ten minutes from now, it's all supposed to end at the OK Corral. Very well—we are not going to be there. We are going to sit right here. We are not going to move from this spot."

Spock nodded slowly, but he was frowning. The others braced themselves, as if daring anyone to move them.

*Flip!*

Sunlight blazed upon them from a low angle. They were in the OK Corral.

"Let's get out of here!" Kirk said. He vaulted over the fence, hearing the others thump to the ground after him, and dashed into an alley. At the other end, he paused to reconnoiter.

Ahead was the corral, with a wagon box and several horses tied in front of it. Kirk started, momentarily stunned.

"Must have gotten turned around," he said. "This way."

He led the way back up the alley. Its far end debouched onto the main street. They crossed quickly into another alley, jogging, watching the blank wooden buildings that hemmed them in.

At the end of the alley was the OK Corral.

"They're breeding like pups," Scotty said.

"Down that way . . ."

But 'down that way' also ended at the OK Corral.

"They've got us," Kirk said stonily. "The Melkotians don't mean for us to miss this appointment. All right. Remember that these guns are heavier than phasers. Pull them straight up—and drag them *down* into line the minute you've fired off the first shot."

"Captain," Spock said, "that is suicide. We are none of us skilled in the use of these weapons. Nor can we avoid the OK Corral, that is quite clear. But—very quickly—let me ask you, what killed Ensign Chekov?"

"Mr. Spock, he was killed by a bullet."

"No, Captain. He was killed by his own mind. Listen

33

to me, please; this is urgent. The failure of Dr. McCoy's drug was the clue. *This place is unreal.* It is a telepathic forgery by the Melkotians. Nothing that happens here is real. Nothing at all."

"Chekov is dead," McCoy said grimly.

"In this environment, yes. Elsewhere—we cannot know. We can judge reality only by the responses of our senses. Once we are convinced of the reality of a given situation, our minds abide by its rules: the guns are solid, the bullets are real, they can kill. But only because we believe it!"

"I see the Earps coming toward us," Kirk said. "And they look mighty convincing—and deadly. So do their guns. Do you think you can protect us just by disbelieving in them?"

"I can't protect anybody but myself, Captain; you must entertain your own disbelief—totally. One single doubt, and you will die."

The three Earps, side by side, black-clad and grim, walked slowly down the street, their faces expressionless. Pedestrians scurried away from them like startled quail.

"Mr. Spock," Kirk said, "we can't turn disbelief on and off like clockwork. I know you can; but we're just human beings."

"The Vulcanian mind meld," Dr. McCoy said suddenly.

"Yes, Dr. McCoy. I could not have suggested it myself; I have cultural blocks against invading another man's mind. But if you will risk it . . ."

"I will."

McCoy hesitated. Then he stepped back until his back was against the wagon box. Spock came to him, closer and closer, his fingers spreading. Face to face, closer and closer.

"Your mind to my mind," Spock said softly. "Your thoughts to my thoughts. Listen to me, Bones. Be with me. Be one with me."

McCoy closed his eyes, and then slowly, opened them again.

The three Earps had been joined by Doc Holliday. He was holding a double-barreled, sawed-off shotgun under his frock coat. He fell in step with the brothers. Funereal in look and aspect, grim and unsmiling, rhythmic as a

34

burial procession, they came down the street, real, the quintessence of death.

Spock's fingers moved to Kirk's face. "They are unreal —without body," he whispered. "Listen to me, Jim. Be with me. They are only illusion, shadows without substance. They cannot affect you. My heart to your heart, I promise you."

The Earps and Holliday marched on across the lengthening shadows. The shotgun barrel swung periodically under Holliday's coattails. Their cheeks were hollow, their eyes dark as pitch. The street behind them was frozen, and the sky was darkening.

"Scotty," Spock said, his voice suddenly taking on a dark, Caledonian color, as deep as that of a prophet's. "Listen to me. Clouds these are without water, carried about by winds. They are trees whose fruit withereth, twice dead, plucked up by the roots; wandering stars, to whom is reserved the blackness of eternity, forever."

The spectral stalkers halted, perhaps ten paces away. Wyatt Earp said, "Draw."

Kirk looked at his people. Their expressions were glassy, faraway, strange, like lambs awaiting the slaughter. With a slight nod, he dropped his hand toward his gunbutt.

The Earps drew. It seemed as though twenty pistol shots rang out in as many seconds—two shotgun blasts—another pistol shot. The street fogged with the smoke and stench of black powder. Every single shot had come from the Earps' side.

"Thank you, Mr. Spock," Kirk said tranquilly, staring into the eyes of the astonished gunmen. "And now, gentlemen, if you please, let's finish this up—fast, hard and good."

The four from the *Enterprise* moved in on the Earps. The gunmen were accustomed to shoot-outs and to pistol-whipping and to barroom brawls; but against advanced space-age karate techniques and Spock's delicately precise knowledge of the human nervous system's multiple vulnerabilities, they had no defense whatsoever. Within moments, 'history' was a welter of unconcious black-clad bodies in the dust . . .

. . . And Tombstone, Arizona, wavered, pulsed, faded, and vanished into a foggy limbo.

In the fog, Kirk became aware that Chekov was standing beside him. He had to swallow twice before he could manage to say, "Welcome back, Ensign."

He had no time to say more, for the transparent figure of the Melkot was forming against the eerie backdrop of the mists.

"Explain," the Melkot said.

"Glad to," Kirk said, in a voice far from friendly. "What would you like explained?"

"To you the bullets were unreal. To the players we put against you, the bullets were real, and would kill. But you did not kill them."

"We kill only in self-defense," Kirk said. "Once we saw that it was unnecessary to kill your players, we protected ourselves less wastefully, on all sides."

"Is this," the Melkot said, "the way of your kind?"

"By and large. We are not all alike. But in general, we prefer peace—and I speak not only for my species, but for a vast alliance of fellow creatures who subscribe to the same tenets. We were sent here to ask you to join it."

There was a long silence. And as they waited, the familiar fading effect began again—and then they were on the bridge of the *Enterprise*.

Uhura was at her post. She did not seem at all surprised to see them. In fact, her manner was so matter-of-fact as to suggest that they had never left at all.

Chekov began to react, but Kirk held up his hand in warning. Puzzled, Chekov said in a low voice, "Captain—what happened? Where have I been?"

"Where do you think?"

"Why—right here, it seems. But I remember a girl . . ."

"Nothing else?"

"No," Chekov said. "But she seemed so real . . ."

"Perhaps that explains why you're here. Nothing else was real to you."

Chekov looked more baffled than ever, but evidently decided to leave well enough alone.

"Captain," Lt. Uhura said, "I'm getting a transmission from the Melkot buoy."

"Cycle it for sixty seconds. Mr. Spock, has any time elapsed since the—uh—last time we all sat here?"

"The clock says not, Captain."

36

"I suspected not. Did it happen?"

"I cannot give a yes or no answer, Captain. It is a matter of interpretation."

"All right, Lt. Uhura. Let's hear what the Melkotian buoy has to say."

The buoy said: "Aliens! You have entered the space of the Melkot. We welcome you and promise peaceful contact."

"Very good. Lt. Uhura, ask them to specify a meeting place. Mr. Spock, a word with you in private, please."

Spock obediently drew to one side of the bridge with his Captain.

"Mr. Spock, once again we owe you our thanks for quick, thorough and logical thinking. But I will tell you something else. Privately, and for no other ears than yours, I think you are a sentimental bag of mush."

"Sir!"

"I heard what you said to me, and to the other men, when you were convincing us not to believe in the Melkotian illusions. Every word was based upon the most intimate understanding of each man involved—understanding —and honest love."

"Captain," Spock said, from behind his mask, "I did what was necessary."

"Of course you did. Very well, Mr. Spock—carry on."

But as Spock went stiffly back to his library-computer, the commandatorial eyes which followed him were not without a certain glitter of amusement.

# THE DOOMSDAY MACHINE*

## (Norman Spinrad)

Shock after shock. First, the distress call from the *Constellation,* a starship of the same class as the *Enterprise,* and commanded by Brand Decker, one of Kirk's oldest classmates; a call badly garbled, and cut off in the middle.

The call seemed to have come from the vicinity of M-370, a modest young star with a system of seven planets. But when the *Enterprise* arrived in the system, the *Constellation* was not there—and neither was the system.

The star had not gone nova; it was as placid as it had always been. But of the planets there was nothing left but asteroids, rubble and dust.

Lt. Uhura tried to project the line of the distress call. The line led through four more former solar systems—*all* now nothing but asteroids, rubble and dust . . . No, not quite: The two inner planets of the fifth system appeared to be still intact—and from somewhere near where the third planet should have been, they heard once more the weak beacon of the *Constellation,* no longer signaling distress, but black disaster.

The beacon was automatic; no voice came from her despite repeated calls. And when they found her, the viewscreen showed that two large, neat holes, neat as phaser cuts, had been drilled through her warp-drive pods.

Kirk called a yellow alert at once, though there was no sign of a third ship in the area, except for some radio

---

*Hugo Award nominee

interference which might easily be sunspots. Scott reported that all main and auxiliary power plants aboard the *Constellation* were dead, but that the batteries were operative at a low level. Her life support systems were operative, too, also at a very low level, except for the bridge area, which—as the viewscreen showed—was badly damaged and uninhabitable.

"We'll board," Kirk said. "The *Constellation* packed as much firepower as we do; I want to know what could cut a starship up like that. And there may be a few survivors. Bones, grab your kit. Scotty, select a damage control party and come with us. Mr. Spock, you'll stay here and maintain Yellow Alert."

"Acknowledge," Spock said.

Aboard the *Constellation,* the lights were weak and flickering, and wreckage littered the deck. The three crewmen of the damage control party found the radiation level normal, the air pressure eleven pounds per square inch, the communications system shorted out, the filtration system dead. The warp drive was a hopeless pile of junk. Surprisingly, the reactor was intact—it had simply been shut down—and the impulse drive was in fair shape.

But there were no survivors—and no bodies.

Kirk thought this over a moment, then called the *Enterprise.* "Mr. Spock, this ship appears abandoned. Could the crew have beamed down to one of those two planets?"

"Improbable, Captain," Spock's voice replied. "The surface temperature on the inner planet is roughly that of molten lead, and the other has a poisonous, dense atmosphere resembling that of Venus."

"All right, we'll keep looking. Kirk out."

"The phaser banks are almost exhausted," Scott reported. "They didn't give her up without a battle."

"But *where are they?* I can't understand a man like Brand Decker abandoning his ship as long as his life support systems were operative."

"The computer system is still intact. If the screen on the engineers' bridge is still alive, we might get a playback of the Captain's log."

"Good idea. Let's go."

The screen on the engineers' bridge was in fact dead,

but they forgot this almost the moment they noticed it; for seated before the console, staring at the useless instruments, was Commodore Brand Decker. His uniform was tattered, his hair mussed.

"Commodore Decker!"

Decker looked up blankly. He seemed to have trouble focusing on Kirk. McCoy was quickly beside him.

"Commodore—what happened to your ship?"

"Ship?" Decker said. "Attacked . . . that thing . . . fourth planet breaking up . . ."

"Jim, he's in a state of shock," McCoy said. "No pressure on him now, please."

"Very well. Do what you can for him here. We've got to question him."

"He mentioned the fourth planet," Scott said. "There are only two left now."

"Yes. Pull the last microtapes from the sensor memory bank and beam them across to Spock. I want a full analysis of all reports of what happened when they went in on that planet."

"I've given this man a tranquilizer," McCoy said. "You can try a few questions now. But take it easy."

Kirk nodded. "Commodore, I'm Jim Kirk, in command of the *Enterprise*. Do you understand?"

"*Enterprise?*" Decker said. "We couldn't contact— couldn't run—had to do it—no choice at all . . ."

"No choice about what?"

"I had to beam them down. The only chance they had . . ."

"Do you mean your crew?"

Decker nodded. "I was—last aboard. It attacked again —knocked out the transporter. I was stranded aboard."

"But *where* was the crew?"

"The third planet."

"There is no third planet now."

"There was," Decker said. "There *was*. That thing . . . destroyed it . . . I heard them . . . four hundred of my men . . . calling for help . . . begging me . . . and I couldn't . . ." The Commodore's voice went slower and slower, as though he were an ancient clockwork mechanism running down, and faded out entirely.

"Fantastic," Scott said, almost to himself. "What kind of a weapon could do that?"

"If you had seen it—you'd know," Decker said, rousing himself with obvious effort. "The whole thing is a weapon. It must be."

Kirk said, "What does it look like, Commodore?"

"A hundred times the size of a starship—a mile long, with a maw big enough to swallow a dozen ships. It destroys planets—cuts them to rubble."

"Why? Is it an alien ship—or is it alive?"

"Both—neither—I don't know."

"Where is this thing now?"

"I—don't know that either."

Kirk lifted his communicator. "Mr. Spock, still no sign of any other vessel in the vicinity?"

"Well, yes and no, Captain," the First Officer replied. "The subspace radio interference is now so heavy as to cut us off from Starfleet Command; obviously it cannot be sunspots. But our sensors still show only the *Constellation.*"

"How is the tape analysis going?"

"We're ready now, Captain. We find that the *Constellation* was attacked by what seems to be essentially a robot—an automated weapon of great size and power. Its apparent function is to smash planets to rubble, and then 'digest' the debris for fuel. It is, therefore, self-maintaining as long as there are planetary bodies to feed it."

"Origin?"

"Mr. Sulu has computed the path of the machine, using the destroyed solar systems detected by ourselves and the *Constellation* as a base course. We find the path leads out of the galaxy at a sharp angle. Projected in the opposite direction, and assuming that the machine does not alter its course, it will go through the most densely populated section of our galaxy."

"Thank you, Mr. Spock. Maintain Yellow Alert and stand by. Commodore Decker, you've had a rough time. I think it would be best if you and Dr. McCoy beam back to my ship for a physical examination."

"Very well," Decker said. "But you heard your First Officer, Captain. That thing is heading for the heart of our galaxy—thousands of populated planets! *What are you going to do?*"

"I'm going to think," Kirk said. "Mr. Spock, have the Transporter Room beam Dr. McCoy and Commodore Decker aboard immediately."

A moment later, the two men shimmered out of existence, leaving no one but Kirk and Scott on the dead engineers' bridge.

"They're aboard, Captain," Spock's voice said from the communicator. And then, without any transition at all, "Red alert! Red Alert! Mr. Sulu, out of the plane of the ecliptic at sixty degrees north! Warp One!"

"Mr. Spock!" Kirk shouted, although of course Spock could have heard him equally well if he had whispered. "Why the alert? Why are you running? I'm blind here."

"Commodore Decker's planet-killer, Captain. It just popped out of subspace. Metallic body, a large funnel-mouth, at least a mile long. It is pursuing us, but we seem to be able to maintain our distance at Warp One. No, it's gaining on us. Sensors indicate some kind of total conversion drive. No evidence of life aboard. Which is not surprising, since isotope dating indicates that it is at least three billion years old."

"Three *billion!*" Kirk said. "Mr. Spock, since it's a robot, what are our chances of deactivating it?"

"I would say none, Captain. I doubt that we would be able to maneuver close enough without drawing a direct attack upon ourselves. We could of course beam men aboard in spacesuits, but since the thing is obviously designed to be a doomsday machine, its control mechanisms would be inaccessible on principle."

"A doomsday machine, sir?" Scott said.

"A calculated bluff, Scotty. A weapon so powerful that it will destroy both sides in a war if it's used. Evidently some race in another galaxy built one—this one—and its bluff was called. The machine is now all that's left of the race—and it's evidently programmed to keep on destroying planets as long as it's functioning."

"Well, whatever happens, we can't let it go beyond us to the next solar system. We have to stop it here. You'd better . . ."

He was interrupted by the filtered sound of a concussion.

"Mr. Spock!" a distant voice called. It sounded like Uhura. "We've taken a hit! The transporter's out!"

"Emergency power on screens. Maximum evasive action! Phaser banks . . ."

And then the communicator went dead.

"Spock! Come in! Spock!" It was useless. "Scotty—we're stuck here. Deaf and blind."

"Worse than that, Captain. We're paralyzed, too. The warp drive is just so much wreckage."

"We can't just sit here while that thing attacks our ship. Forget the warp drive and get me some impulse power—half-power, quarter-power, anything I can maneuver with, even if you have to get out and push."

"But we'd never be able to outrun . . ."

"We're going to fight the thing, not outrun it," Kirk said grimly. "If we can get this hulk going, we may be able to distract the robot, and give the *Enterprise* a better chance to strike at it. Get cracking, Scotty. I'm going to see what I can do with this viewscreen. We can't move until I can see where we're going."

Seated in the Captain's chair, Spock evaluated the damage. Warp and impulse drives were still operative. As he checked, Commodore Decker and McCoy watched him tensely.

"Communications?"

"Under repair, Mr. Spock," Uhura said.

"Transporter?"

Sulu said, "Also under repair."

"Hmm," Spock said. "Random factors seem to have operated in our favor."

"In plain, non-Vulcan English," McCoy said, "we've been lucky."

"Isn't that what I said, Doctor?" Spock said blandly.

"The machine's veering off," Sulu reported. "It's back on its old course. Next in line is the Rigel system."

"No doubt programmed to ignore anything as small as a ship beyond a certain radius," Spock said. "Mr. Sulu, circle back so we can pick up the Captain while we effect repairs. We may have to take the *Constellation* in tow . . ."

"You can't let that thing reach Rigel!" Decker broke in. "Millions of innocent people . . ."

"I am aware of the population of the Rigel colonies, Commodore, but we are only one ship. Our deflector generators are strained. Our radio is useless as long as we are in the vicinity of the robot. Logic dictates that our primary duty is to survive to warn Starfleet Command."

"Our primary duty is to maintain the life and safety of Federation planets! Helmsman, belay that last order! Track and close on that machine!"

Sulu looked questioningly at Spock. It was a difficult problem. Kirk had left Spock in command, but Decker was the senior officer aboard. Spock said evenly, "Carry out my last order, Mr. Sulu."

"Mr. Spock," Decker said, "I'm formally notifying you that I am exercising my option under regulations as senior officer to assume command of the *Enterprise*. That thing has got to be destroyed."

"You attempted to destroy it before, sir," Spock said, "and it resulted in a wrecked ship and a dead crew. Clearly a single ship cannot combat that machine."

Decker winced, then stabbed a finger at Spock. "That will be all, Mr. Spock. You're relieved of command. Don't force me to relieve you of duty as well."

Spock got up. McCoy grabbed his arm. "Spock, you can't let him do this!"

"Unfortunately," Spock said, "Starfleet Order one-zero-four, Section B, reads, Paragraph A, 'In the absence of the . . .' "

"To blazes with regulations! How can you let him take command when you *know* he's wrong?"

"If you can officially certify Commodore Decker medically or psychologically unfit to command, I may relieve him under Section C."

"I can't do that," McCoy said. "He's as sound as any of us. I can say his present plan is crazy, but medically I'd have to classify that as a difference of opinion, not a diagnosis."

"Mr. Spock knows his duties under the regulation," Decker said. "Do you, Doctor?"

"Yes, sir," McCoy said disgustedly. "To go to Sickbay and wait for the casualties you're about to send me." He stalked out.

"Hard about and close," Decker said. "Full emergency power on deflectors. Stand by on main phaser banks."

On the viewscreen, the planet-killer began to grow in size. Decker stared at it with grim intensity, as though the combat to come was to be a personal one, hand-to-hand.

"In range, sir," Sulu reported.

"Fire phasers!"

The beams lanced out. It was a direct hit—but there seemed to be no effect at all. The beams simply bounced off.

In answer, a pencil of solid blue light leapt out of the maw of the planet-killer. The *Enterprise* seemed to stagger, and for a moment all the lights went down.

"Whew!" Sulu said. "What *is* that thing?"

"It's an anti-proton beam," Decker said in an abstracted voice. "It's what the machine cut the fourth planet up with."

"The deflectors weren't built to take it, sir," Spock said. "The next time, the generators may blow."

Decker paid no attention. "Keep closing and maintain phaser fire."

Spock studied his instruments. "Sir," he said, "sensors indicate that the robot's hull is neutronium—collapsed matter so dense that a cubic inch of it would weigh a ton. We could no more get a phaser beam through it than we could a matchstick. If we could somehow get a clear shot at the internal mechanism . . ."

"Now that's more like it, Mr. Spock. We'll cut right across the thing's funnel and ram a phaser beam down its throat. Helmsman, change course to intercept."

Sulu shifted the controls cautiously, obviously expecting another blow from the anti-proton beam; but evidently the monstrous mechanism had no objection to having this morsel sailing directly into its maw.

"Fire!"

The phasers cut loose. Sulu studied the screen intently.

"Those beams are just bouncing around inside," he reported. "We can't get a shot straight through."

"Close in."

45

"Sir," Spock said, "any closer and that anti-proton beam will go through our deflectors like tissue paper."

"We'll take the chance. Thousands of planets are at stake."

"Sir, there is no chance at all. It is pure suicide. And attempted suicide would be proof that you are psychologically unfit to command. Unless you give the order to veer off, I will relieve you on that basis."

"Vulcan logic!" Decker said in disgust. "Blackmail would be a more honest word. All right, helmsman, veer off—emergency impulse power."

"Commodore," Sulu said in a strained voice, "I can't veer off. That thing's got some kind of a tractor beam on us."

"Can it pull us in?"

"No, sir, we can manage a stand-off, for perhaps seven hours. In the meantime it can take pot shots at us whenever it likes."

On the engineers' bridge of the *Constellation*, the viewscreen finally lit. Kirk stared at what it showed with shock and disbelief. A gasp from behind him told him that Scott had just entered the bridge.

"Is Spock out of his mind?"

"I don't understand it either—I ordered evasive action. What's the situation below?"

"We've got the screens up, but they won't last more than a few hours, and they can't take a beating. As for the impulse drive, the best I can give you is one-third power. And at that I'll have to nurse it."

"Go ahead then. We've got to break up that death-dance out there somehow." As Scott left, Kirk once more tried his communicator. To his gratification, he got Lt. Uhura at once; evidently the *Enterprise*, too, had been making repairs. "Lieutenant, give me Mr. Spock, fast."

But the next voice said: *"Enterprise* to Kirk. Commodore Decker here."

"Decker? What's going on? Give me Mr. Spock!"

"I'm in command here, Captain. According to regulations, I assumed command on finding Mr. Spock reluctant to take proper action . . ."

46

"You mean you're the lunatic responsible for almost destroying my ship? Mr. Spock, if you can hear me, I give you a direct order to answer me."

"Spock here, Captain."

"Good. On my personal authority as Captain of the *Enterprise*, I order you to relieve Commodore Decker. Commodore, you may file a formal protest of the violation of regulations involved with Starfleet Command—if any of us live to reach a star base. In the meantime, Mr. Spock, if the Commodore resists being relieved, place him under arrest. Is that clear?"

"Not only is it clear," Spock's voice said, "but· I have just done so. Your further orders, sir?"

"Get away from that machine!"

"Sir, we can't; we have been pegged by a tractor. The best we can do is prevent ourselves from being pulled inside it, for about the next six point five hours—or until it decides to shoot at us again."

"I was afraid of that. All right, I'm going to move the *Constellation* into your vicinity and see if I can distract the machine. With the power I've got available, it will take at least three hours. Is your transporter working again, too?"

"Yes, sir, but I assure you that you'd be no safer here than there."

"I'm aware of that, Mr. Spock. I just want to be sure you can beam me aboard once we're in range, so I can take command personally from the Commodore if he gives you any trouble. That's all for now. Kirk out."

Kirk set the *Constellation* in creaking motion and then thought a while. Finally he called Scott.

"How's the drive holding up, Scotty?"

"Under protest, I would say, sir," Scott responded. "But if you don't demand any violent maneuvers I think it'll stay in one piece."

"Very well. Now I need an engineering assessment. What would happen if the reactor were to go critical?"

"Why, Captain, you know as well as I do—a fusion explosion, of course."

"Yes, Scotty, but if *this* reactor were to do so, how big would the explosion be?"

"Oh," Scott's voice said. "That's easily answered, the potential is always on the faceplate of a ship's reactor; I'll just check it . . . The figure is 97.8 megatons."

"Would the resulting fireball be sufficient to disrupt a neutronium hull?"

"Neutronium, sir? You mean the planet-killer? What makes you think the hull is neutronium?"

"Because from this distance the *Enterprise* could have cut it into scrap metal by now if it weren't."

"Hmm—aye, that follows. Well, Captain, neutronium is formed in the cores of white dwarf stars, with fusion going on all around it. So I'd say the fireball would just push the machine away, rather than collapsing the hull. And sir, in a vacuum the fireball would be something like a hundred and fifty miles in diameter. That means it would envelop the *Enterprise* too—and *we* don't have a neutronium hull."

"That's true, but it isn't what I have in mind. Scotty, I want you to rig a thirty-second delayed detonation switch, so the reactor can be blown from up here on the engineers' bridge. Can do?"

"Aye, sir," Scott said. "But why . . ."

"Just rig it, fast. Then get yourself and the damage control party up here. Kirk to *Enterprise*."

"Spock here."

"Mr. Spock, I don't have any sensors over here worth mentioning, so I won't know when I'm in transporter range. The instant I am, let me know."

"Acknowledge. May I ask your intent, Captain?"

"Scotty is rigging a thirty-second delayed detonation switch on the impulse power reactor of the *Constellation*. I am going to pilot the vessel right down the planet-killer's throat—and you'll have thirty seconds to beam the five of us aboard the *Enterprise* before the reactor blows."

There was a brief pause. When Spock's voice returned, there actually seemed to be a faint trace of human concern in it. "Jim, thirty seconds is very fine timing. The transporter is not working at a hundred per cent efficiency; our repairs were necessarily rather hasty."

"That's a chance I'll have to take. However, it does change things a little. I'll want you to beam Mr. Scott and the damage control party over as soon as we are in range. I'll be the only one to stay aboard until the last minute."

"Acknowledge. Sir, may I point out two possible other flaws?"

While Spock was talking, Scott came into the room carrying a small black box. Mounted on it was a single three-position knife switch—that is, one with two slots for the blade, the third position being disengaged from either. He set it down on the panel in front of Kirk.

"Go ahead, Mr. Spock, your advice is half your value. Where are the flaws?"

"First, we cannot know the composition of the interior workings of the planet-killer. If they too are neutronium, nothing will happen except that it will get very hot inside there."

" 'Very hot' is certainly a mild way of putting it," Kirk said drily. "All right, Mr. Spock, to use logic right back at you, Proposition A: The planet-killer operates in a vacuum, which means most of its circuits are cryogenic. Heating them a few million degrees may be quite enough to knock it out. Proposition B: Pure neutronium cannot carry an elecrical current, because its electron shells are collapsed. Hence, many important parts of the planet-killer's interior cannot be neutronium. Conclusion: an interior fusion explosion will kill it. How is that for a syllogism?"

"It is not a syllogism at all, Captain, but a sorites; however, I agree that it is a sound one. My second objection is more serious. The planet-killer is open to space at one end, and that is the end facing us. The neutronium hull will confine the fireball and shoot it directly out of the funnel at the *Enterprise* in a tongue of flame hundreds of miles long. This is an undesirable outcome."

Kirk almost laughed, although there was nothing in the least funny about the objection itself. "Mr. Spock, if that happens, we will all die. But the planet-killer will have been destroyed. Our mandate is to protect Federation lives, property and interests. Hence this outcome, as you call it, is in fact more desirable than undesirable."

"Now that," Spock said, "*is* a syllogism, and a sound one. Very well, Captain, I withdraw my objections."

When Kirk put down the communicator, he found Scott

49

staring at him ruefully. "Your sense of humor," the engineer said ruefully, "comes out at the oddest times. Well, there is your detonator, Captain. When you pull the switch into the *up* position, it's armed. When you push it down into the other slot, you have thirty seconds until *blooey!*"

"Simple enough."

"Captain," Spock's voice came again. "The *Constellation* has just come within transporter range. However, when you are ready to have your party beam over, I suggest that you leave the bridge. We do not have fine enough control to pick four men out of five, and even if we did, we would not know which four of the five until it was too late."

"Very well, Mr. Spock. I will leave the bridge; make your pickup in sixty seconds."

He got up. As he was at the door, Scott said, "Take care, Jim."

"Scotty, I don't *want* to die, I assure you."

When he returned, the engineers' bridge was empty; but Scott's voice was still there. It was coming from the communicator, and it was using some rather ungentlemanly language.

"Scotty, what's the matter? Are you all right?"

"Aye, I'm all right, skipper, and so are we all—but the transporter blew under the load. I dinna ken hae lang it'll take to fix it."

The return of Scott's brogue told Kirk how serious the situation actually was. Kirk did not even say, "Well, do your best." It was unnecessary.

The next few hours were an almost intolerable mixture of loneliness and tension, while the monstrous shape of the planet-killer and its mothlike captive grew slowly on the screen.

Yet not once in all this time did the robot again fire its anti-proton beam, which probably would have gone through the *Enterprise* like a knife through cheese; the ship was using almost all her power in fighting against the tractor ray. That, Kirk supposed, was a present given them by the nature of machine intelligence; the robot, having settled on the course of drawing the *Enterprise* into

50

itself—and, probably, having estimated that in such a struggle it could not lose, eventually—saw no reason to take any other action.

"Mr. Spock?"

"Yes, Captain."

"Don't fire on that thing again. Don't do *anything* to alter present circumstances—not even sneeze."

"I follow you, Captain. If we do not change the parameters, the machine mindlessly maintains the equation."

"Well, that's what I hope. How is the transporter coming?"

"Slowly. Mr. Scott says half its resistors are burned out. They are easy to replace individually, but so many is a time-consuming task."

"Computation?"

"We may have a most unreliable repair done when the *Constellation* is within a hundred miles of the robot. Sir, we also compute that one hundred miles is the limit of the robot's defensive envelope, inside which it takes offensive action against moving objects under power."

"Well, I can't very well shut off power. Let's just hope it's hungry."

The funnel swelled, much faster now. Kirk checked his watch, then poised his hand over the switch.

"Mr. Spock, I'm running out of time myself. Any luck now on the transporter?"

"It may work, Captain. I can predict no more."

"All right. Stand by."

The funnel now covered the entire star field; nothing else was to be seen but that metal throat. Still the robot had not fired.

"All right, Spock! Beam me aboard!"

He threw the switch. An instant later, the engineers' bridge of the doomed *Constellation* faded around him, and he found himself in the Transporter Room of the *Enterprise*. He raced to the nearest auxiliary viewscreen. Over the intercom, Spock's voice was counting: "Twenty-five seconds to detonation. Computer, mark at ten seconds and give us a fiftieth of a second warp drive at Warp One at second zero point five."

This order baffled Kirk for an instant; then he realized

that he was *still* looking down the throat of the doomsday machine, and that Spock was hoping to make a short subspace jump away the instant the robot's tractor apparatus was consumed—if it was.

"Fifteen seconds. *Mark.* Five seconds. Four. Three. Two. One."

*Flick!*

Suddenly, on the auxiliary screen, the doomsday machine was thousands of miles away. The screen zoomed up the magnification to restore the image.

As it did so, a spear of intolerable light grew out of the mouth of the funnel. Promptly, Kirk ran for the elevators and the control room.

A silent group was watching the main viewscreen, including Commodore Decker. The tongue of flame was still growing. It now looked to be at least two hundred miles long. It would have consumed the *Enterprise* like a midge.

Then, gradually, it faded. Spock checked his board.

"Did it work?" Kirk demanded.

"I cannot tell yet, Captain. The radiation from the blast itself is too intense. But the very fact that we broke away indicates at least some damage . . . Ah, the radiation is decaying. Now we shall see."

Kirk held his breath.

"Decay curve inflecting," Spock said. "The shape—yes, the curve is now exponential. All energy sources are deactivated. Captain, it is dead."

There was a pandemonium of cheering. Under cover of the noise, Decker moved over to Kirk.

"My last command," he said in a low voice. "But you were right, Captain Kirk. My apologies for usurping your command."

"You acted to save Federation lives and property, as I did. If you in turn are willing to drop your complaint against my overriding regulations—which you have every right to make—we'll say no more about it."

"Of course I'll drop it. But the *Constellation* is nevertheless my last command. I cannot forget that my first attempt to attack that thing cost four hundred lives—men who trusted me—and that I had the bad judgment to try it again with *your* men's lives. When a man stops learning, he's no longer fit to command."

"That," Kirk said, "is a judgment upon yourself that only you can make. My opinion is that it is a wise and responsible judgment. But it is only an opinion. Mr. Sulu?"

"Sir?"

"Let's get the dancing in the streets over with, and lay a course for Star Base Seventeen."

"Yes, sir." But the helmsman could not quite stop grinning. Spock, of course, never grinned, but he was looking, if possible, even more serious than usual.

"Mr. Spock, you strike me as a man who still has some reservations."

"Only one, Captain; and it is pure speculation."

"Nevertheless, let's hear it."

"Well, Captain, when two powers prepare forces of such magnitude against each other, it almost always means that they are at a state of technological parity; otherwise they would not take such risks of self-destruction."

"Meaning?"

"Meaning, sir, that the existence of one such doomsday machine implies the existence of another."

"I suppose that's possible," Kirk said slowly, repressing a shudder. "Though the second one may not have been launched in time. Well, Mr. Spock, supposing we were to hear of another? What would you do?"

Spock's eyebrows went up. "That is no problem, sir. I would feed it a fusion bomb disguised as a ship, or better still, an asteroid; that is not what concerned me. The danger, as such, can now be regarded as minimal, even if there *is* another such machine."

"Then if you weren't thinking of the danger, what *were* you thinking of?"

"Of the nuisance," Spock said. "Having to deal with the same problem twice is untidy; it wastes time."

Kirk thought back to those hours aboard the haunted hulk of the *Constellation*—and of the four hundred dead men on the devoured planet.

"I," he said, "prefer my problems tidy. It saves lives."

# ASSIGNMENT: EARTH

## (Gene Roddenberry and Art Wallace)

Kirk viewed the conversion—however temporary and partial—of the *Enterprise* into a time machine with considerable misgivings. He had to recognize, of course, that an occasional assignment of this kind had become inevitable, the moment the laboratory types had had a chance to investigate the reports of the time-travel he, Spock and McCoy had been subjected to from the City on the edge of Forever, and the time-warp the whole ship had run into when it had hit the black star.

But these two experiences had only made him more acutely aware of the special danger of time-travel: the danger that the tiniest of false moves could change the future—or what was for Kirk the present—and in the process wipe out Kirk, the *Enterprise,* the Federation itself. Hovering in orbit above the Earth of 1969, even in hiding behind deflector screens, was a hair-trigger situation.

For that matter, that was why they were here, for 1969 had been a hair-trigger year. In Kirk's time, nobody really understood how the Earth had survived it. In the terrible scramble with which the year had ended, crucial documents had been lost; still others, it was strongly suspected, had been falsified. And it was not just the historians, but the Federation itself, that wanted to know the answers. They were possibly of military as well as political interest, and in a galaxy that contained the Klingon Empire as well as the Federation, they might be a good deal more than interesting.

Which explained the vast expense of sending a whole starship back in time to monitor Earth communications. Nevertheless . . .

His musings were interrupted by a faint but unmistakable shuddering of the deck of the bridge beneath his feet. What on Earth . . .

"Alert status," he snapped. "Force shields maximum. Begin sensor scan. Any station with information, report."

Immediately the telltale light for the Transporter Room went on and Kirk flipped the intercom switch.

"Spock here, Captain. We are having transporter trouble; Mr. Scott just called me down to help."

"You shouldn't be using the transporter at all!"

"Nobody was, Captain. It went on by itself and we find we cannot shut it off. We seem accidentally to have intercepted someone else's transporter beam—and one a great deal more powerful than ours."

"Mr. Spock, you know as well as I do that the twentieth century had no such device—" Again he was interrupted by the faint shudder. Spock's voice came back urgently:

"Nevertheless, Captain, someone—or something—is beaming aboard this vessel."

"I'll be right down."

In the Transporter Room, Kirk found the situation as reported. All circuits were locked open; nothing Spock or Scott could do would close them. The familiar shimmering effect was already beginning in the transporter chamber.

"For all its power," Spock said, "that beam is originating at least a thousand light years away."

"Which," Scott added, "is a good deal farther than any transporter beam of our *own* century could reach."

The ship shuddered again, more strongly than before. "Stop fighting it," Kirk said quietly. "Set up our own field for it and let it through. Obviously we'll have serious damage otherwise."

"Aye, sir," Scott said. He worked quickly.

The shimmering grew swiftly in brightness. A haze form appeared in it, and gradually took on solidity. Kirk stared, his jaw dropped.

The figure they had pulled in from incredibly deep space was that of a man impeccably dressed in a twentieth-century business suit. Nor was this all: in his arms he carried a sleek black cat, wearing a necklace collar of glittering white stones.

"Security detail," Kirk said. "On the double."

The stranger seemed as startled as Kirk was. He looked about the Transporter Room in baffled anger, rubbing the huge cat soothingly. The exotic element in no way detracted from his obvious personal force; he was tall, rugged, vital.

"Why have you intercepted me?" he said at once. "Please identify yourselves."

"You're aboard the United Spaceship *Enterprise*. I am Captain James Kirk, commanding."

The black cat made a strange sound, rather like one of the many odd noises a Siamese cat can make, and yet somehow also not catlike at all.

"I hear it, Isis," the stranger said. "A space vessel. But from what planet?"

"Earth."

"Impossible! At the present time Earth has no—" his voice trailed off as he became aware of Spock. Then, "Humans with a Vulcan! No wonder! You're from the future!"

He dropped the cat and reached for the control panel in the transporter chamber. "You must beam me down onto Earth immediately. There's not a moment to . . ."

The doors to the Transporter Room snapped open, admitting the ship's security chief and a guard, phasers drawn. At the sight of the weapons the strange man froze. The cat crouched as if for a spring, but the man said instantly, "Careful, Isis. Please listen to me carefully, all of you. My name is Gary Seven. I am a human being of the Twentieth Century. I have been living on another planet, far more advanced than the Earth is. I was beaming from there when you intercepted me."

"Where is the planet?" Kirk said.

"They wish their existence kept secret. In fact, it will remain unknown even in your time."

"It's impossible to hide a whole planet," Scott said.

"Impossible to you; not to them. Captain Kirk, I am of

this time period. You are not. Interfere with me, and with what I must do down there, and you will change history. I am sure you have been thoroughly briefed on the consequence of that."

"I have," Kirk said. "On the other hand, I know nothing about you—even about the truth of anything you've told me."

"We don't have time for that. Every second you delay me is dangerous—this is the most critical year in Earth's history. My planet wants to ensure that Earth survives— an aim which should be of no small interest to you."

Kirk shook his head. "The fact that you know the criticality of the year strongly suggests that you're from the future yourself. It's a risk I can't take until I have more information. I'm afraid I'm going to have to put you in security confinement for the time being."

"You'll regret it."

"Very possibly. Nevertheless, it's what I must do." He gestured to the security chief. The guard bent to pick up the cat, but Gary Seven stepped in his way.

"If you handle Isis," he said, "you will regret *that* even more." He scooped up the cat himself and went out with the security detail.

"I want a special eye kept on that man," Kirk said. "He went along far too docilely. Also, Mr. Spock, ask Dr. McCoy for a fast medical analysis of the prisoner. What I want to know is, is he human? And have the cat checked, too. It may tell us something further about Mr. Seven."

"It seems remarkably intelligent," Spock commented. "As well as strikingly beautiful. All the same, a strange companion to be carrying across a thousand light years on what is supposed to be an urgent mission."

"Exactly. Scotty, could that beam of his have carried him through time as well as space?"

"The theory has always indicated that it's possible," Scott said, "but *we've* never been able to manage it. On the other hand, we've never been able to put that much power into a transporter beam."

"In short, you don't know."

"That's right, sir."

"Very well. See if you can put the machinery back in order. Mr. Spock, please give the necessary orders and then join me on the bridge. We are going to need *lots* of computation."

The computer said: "Present Earth crises fill an entire tape bank, Captain Kirk. The being Gary Seven could be intervening for *or* against Earth in areas of overpopulation, bush wars, revolutions, critically dangerous bacteriological experiments, various emergent hate movements, rising air and water pollution . . ."

"All right, stop," Kirk said. "What specific events are going on today?"

"Excuse me, Captain," Spock said, "but that question will simply open another floodgate. There were half a hundred critical things going on almost every day during 1969. Library, give us the three most heavily weighted of today's events in the danger file."

"There will be an important assassination today," the computer said promptly in its pleasant feminine voice. "An equally dangerous government coup in Asia Minor; and the launching of an orbital nuclear warhead platform by the United States countering a similar launch by a consortium of other powers."

Kirk whistled. "Orbital nuclear devices were one of the greatest worries of this era, as I recall."

"They were," Spock agreed. "Once the sky was full of orbiting H-bombs, the slightest miscalculation could have brought one of them accidentally down and set off a holocaust."

"Sick bay to bridge," the intercom interrupted.

"Kirk here. What is it, Bones?"

"Jim, there isn't any prisoner in the brig. All I found there were the security chief and one guard, both of them acting as if they'd been hypnotized."

"The Transporter Room!" Kirk shouted. "Quick!"

But they were too late. There was nobody in the Transporter Room but a dazed Chief Engineer, and, a moment later, McCoy.

"I was working with my head inside an open panel," Scott said, his voice still a little blurred, "when I heard someone come in. I turned and saw him with the cat under one arm and a thing like a writing stylus pointed at me."

"A miniaturized stunner, no doubt," McCoy said.

"Well, the next thing I knew, I was willing to do anything he asked me to. In fact I beamed him down to Earth myself. Somewhere in the back of my mind I knew I shouldn't, but I did it anyhow."

There was a brief silence.

"And so," Spock said at last, "human or alien, contemporary or future, he has gone to do what he came to do—and we still have no idea what it is."

"We are going to find out," Kirk said. "Scotty, where did you beam him to?"

"That I can't say, Captain. He set the coordinates himself, and put the recorder on wipe. I can give you an estimate, within about a thousand square meters."

"If Spock and I beam down, working from the power consumption data alone, inside that thousand square meters, can you triangulate?"

"Aye, I can do that," Scott said. "It still won't be very precise, but it ought at least to bring you within sighting distance of the man—or whatever he is."

"It is also a major risk to history, Captain," Spock said.

"Which is just why I want you and me to be the ones to go; we had had experience with this kind of operation before. We can't find any answers sitting up here. Have ship's stores prepare proper costumes. Scotty, stand by to beam us down."

The spot where they materialized was a street on New York's upper East Side, not far from the canopied entrance of an elegant apartment building. It was a cold winter day, although there was no snow.

"All right, Scotty," Kirk said into his communicator. "Lock in and check."

"Correlated," Scott's voice said. "Readings indicate a greater altitude—approximately thirty meters higher."

Kirk looked speculatively up the face of the building. Once they entered a maze like that, they might pass within whispering distance of their quarry, behind some door, and never know it.

Nevertheless, they went into the lobby, found an elevator, and went up. At the prescribed heights, they stepped out into a hallway. Nothing but doors.

"Altitude verified, Captain," Scott's voice said. "Proceed forty-one meters, two-four-seven degrees true."

This maneuver wound them up in front of one of the doors, in no way different from any of the others. Kirk and Spock looked at each other. Then Kirk shrugged and pushed the doorbell button, which responded with a melodious chime.

The door was opened by a pretty blonde girl in her early twenties. Kirk and Spock went in, fast.

"Hey, what do you think you're doing?" the girl demanded. "You can't come breaking in . . ."

"Where's Mr. Seven?" Kirk said sharply.

"I don't know who you're talking about!"

Kirk looked around. It was an ordinary Twentieth-Century living room as far as he could see, though perhaps somewhat on the sumptuous side. There was a closed door at the back. Spock pulled out his tricorder and scanned quickly, then pointed at the closed door. "In there, Captain."

They rushed the door, but it was locked. As they tried to voice in, Kirk heard an unfamiliar, brief whirring sound behind him, and then the girl's voice, all in a rush: "Operator, 811 East 68th Street, Apartment 1212, send the police . . ."

Kirk whirled and snatched the phone out of her hand. "No nonsense, Miss. Spock, burn the door open."

The girl gasped as Spock produced his phaser and burned out the entire knob and lock assembly. They rushed in, forcing the girl to come with them.

Here was another large room, also elegantly furnished. One wall was book-lined from a point about a meter from the floor to an equivalent distance from the ceiling. Under a large window was a heavy, ornate desk.

There was no sign of Gary Seven or anybody else. Kirk noted that this seemed to surprise the girl as much as it did himself.

Spock went to the desk, where there was a scatter of papers.

"I'm warning you," the girl said, "I've already called the police."

"Where is Mr. Seven?" Kirk demanded again. "Spock, is she Twentieth Century? Or one of Seven's people?"

"Only Doctor McCoy could establish that, I'm afraid, Captain. But I think you will find these papers interesting. They are plans of the United States government's McKinley Rocket Base."

"Aha. So the orbital platform launching *is* the critical event. Now how long do we . . ."

The doorbell rang. The girl, catching them off guard, dashed for the door. Both men raced after her, Kirk reaching her first. As he grabbed her, she bit his hand, and them screamed.

"Open up in there!" a male voice shouted in the hallway outside. "Police!" Then the door shook to a heavy blow.

Spock too seized the girl. Kirk managed to get his communicator back into play. "Kirk to *Enterprise*. Wide scan, Scotty, we'll be moving. Now!"

Another blow on the door, which burst open. Two policemen lunged in, guns drawn. Spock propelled the girl away from the group toward the library door.

At the same instant, the apartment dissolved and all four of the men—Kirk, Spock, the policemen—were standing in the transporter chamber of the *Enterprise*. The policemen looked about, stunned, but Kirk and Spock raced off the platform instantly.

"Scotty, reverse and energize!"

The policemen faded and vanished.

"Fine, fast work, Scotty."

"That poor girl," Spock said, "is going to have a lot to explain."

"I know it, but we've got something much more important to set right first. Let's have a look at those plans. Blazes, the launch is scheduled in forty minutes! Scotty, look at these. Here's a schematic layout of a rocket base. Can you get it on the viewscreen here?"

"Easy, Captain. In fact, there's an old-style weather satellite in orbit below us; if I can bounce off that, I ought to get good closeups." He moved to the screen. In a moment, he had the base. An enormous, crude multistage rocket was already in launch position, being serviced by something Kirk dimly remembered was called a gantry crane.

"If we could spot your man," Scott added, "I could lock on and beam him up."

"The odds are that he is out of sight," Spock said. "Inside the rocket gantry, or at one of the control centers. I suppose he has a transporter hidden somewhere in that library of his. Otherwise I cannot account for his disappearance, seconds after the tricorder said he was there—or at least, *somebody* was there."

"Surely that base has security precautions," Kirk said.

"So did we," Scott pointed out.

"I see your point, Scotty. All right, continue visual scan, and stand by to beam us down again."

"Won't be necessary, sir. There he is."

And there indeed he was, at the top of the gantry. He had a panel off the side of the rocket and was working feverishly inside it. Nearby sat the black cat, watching with apparent interest.

"Why does he take a pet with him on a dangerous job like that?" Spock said.

"Immaterial now," Kirk said. "Scotty, yank him out of there!"

It was done within seconds. Gary Seven raged, but there was nothing he could do with four phasers leveled on him.

"Relieve him of that hypo and any other hardware he's carrying," Kirk said in a granite voice, "and then take him to the briefing room. This time, Mr. Seven, we are going to get some answers."

"There's no time for that, you fool! The rocket will be launched in nine minutes—and I hadn't finished working on it!"

"Take him along," Kirk said. "And Mr. Spock, put that cat in a separate cabin. Since it's so important for him to have her along, we'll see how well he stands up without her."

Kirk interviewed Seven alone, but with all intercom circuits open, and standing instructions to intervene at discretion and/or report anything that seemed pertinent.

There was no problem about getting Seven to talk. The words came out of him like water from a pressure hose.

"I am what I say I am, a Twentieth-Century human being," he said urgently. "I was one of three agents on

62

Earth. We were equipped with an advanced transporter, and a computer, both hidden behind the bookshelves in my library. I was returned to—where I came from—for final instructions. You intercepted me and caused a critical delay. When I escaped I found both my fellow agents had been killed in a simple automobile accident. I had to work fast, and, necessarily, alone. They need the help, Captain. A rival program of orbital nuclear platforms like this destroyed Omicron III a hundred years ago. It will destroy the Earth if it isn't stopped."

"I don't deny that it's a bad program," Kirk said.

"Then why can't you believe my story? Would a truly advanced planet use force to help Earth? Would they come here in their own strange, alien forms? Nonsense! The best of all possible methods would be to take Earth-born humans to their world, train them for generations, send them back when they're needed."

"The rocket has been launched," Scott's voice responded over the intercom.

"There, you see?" Seven said desperately. "And I hadn't finished working on it. If you can beam me into its warhead I can still . . ."

"Not so fast. What were you going to make it do?"

"I armed the warhead, and gave it a flight path which will bring it down over Southeast Asia."

"What! That'll start a world war in nothing flat!"

"Correction, Captain," Scott's voice said. "The rocket has begun to malfunction, and alerts are being broadcast from capitals all over the world. I would say that the war has effectively started."

"So much for your humanitarian pretenses," Kirk said. "Mr. Scott, prepare to intercept that rocket and beam it out into space somewhere . . ."

"No, no, no!" Seven cried. "That would be a highly conspicuous intervention! It would change history! Captain, I beg of you . . ."

"Excuse me, Captain," said Spock's voice from the intercom. "Please come to the next cabin."

"Mr. Spock, that rocket will impact in something like fifteen minutes. Is this crucial?"

"Absolutely so."

After checking the guards outside the briefing room, Kirk went to the cabin where Spock had taken the cat. The cat was still there, curled up in a chair.

"What's this all about, Mr. Spock?"

"Sir, I have found out why he carries this animal with him wherever he goes, even when it is obviously inconvenient. It changes the entire picture."

"In what way? Spit it out, man!"

"We have all been the victims of a drastic illusion—including Seven. The true fact is, Mr. Seven has been under the closest kind of monitoring during every instant of his activities. I suspected this and bent certain efforts to redisciplining my own mind to see the reality. I can now also do this for you. Look."

He pointed to the chair. Seated in it was a staggeringly beautiful woman. She had long black hair, and wore a sleek black dress and a jeweled choker necklace. Her legs were curled under her with feline grace.

"This," Spock said formally, "is Isis. And now . . ."

The woman was gone; only the cat was there, in a strangely similar position.

"Neither," Spock said, "is likely to be the true form of Mr. Seven's sponsors, but the phenomenon supports the story that he does indeed have sponsors. Whether or not their intentions are malign must be a command decision, and one which I must leave to your human intuition, Captain."

Kirk stared at the illusory cat, which was now washing itself. Then he said, "Mr. Scott!"

"Here, sir."

"Give Mr. Seven back his tools and beam him into the warhead of that rocket—on the double."

The warhead blew at 104 miles. Scott snatched Seven out of it just barely in time.

"You see," Seven told them somewhat later, "it *had* to appear to be a malfunction, which luckily did not do any damage. But it frightened every government on Earth. Already there are signs that nobody will try orbiting such a monster, ever again. So despite your accidental interference from the future, my mission has been completed."

"Correction, Mister Seven," Spock said. "It appears

that we did *not* interfere with history. Rather, the *Enterprise* was simply part of what was supposed to happen on this day in 1969."

Seven looked baffled. Kirk added, "We find in our record tapes that, although it was never generally revealed, on this date a malfunctioning suborbital warhead was detonated *exactly* 104 miles above the Earth. And you'll be pleased that our records show it resulted in a new and stronger international agreement against such weapons."

"I am indeed pleased," Seven said. He picked up the cat. "And now I expect to be recalled. It might save time, Captain, if you would allow me the use of your transporter. I mean no reflection on your technology, but I must get back to my own machine for the trip to—where I am going."

"Of course." Kirk rose. "Mr. Scott, take Mr. Seven to our Transporter Room and beam him down."

At the elevator door, Seven paused. "There is one thing that puzzles me. Your accidental interception, and your tracing me, and your interruption of my work—every one of those events was unplanned and should have produced a major disruption. Yet in each case, it turns out that I made exactly the proper next step to advance the business at hand, even though each time I was working blind. Does the course of history exert that much force on even a single individual?"

Kirk eyed the creature in Seven's arms which, whatever it was, was most certainly not a cat.

"Mr. Seven," he said, "I'm afraid that we in our turn can't tell you *everything* we've learned. The credit for this day's work is largely yours—and I strongly advise you to let it rest at that."

# MIRROR, MIRROR

## (Jerome Bixby)

The Halkan Council was absolutely polite, but its position was rock-hard, and nothing that Kirk, McCoy, Scott or Uhura could say would alter it. The Federation was not to be allowed to mine dilithium crystals on the planet. There was too much potential for destruction in the crystals, and the Halkans would allow nothing to compromise their history of total non-violence. To prevent that, they said, they would die—as a race, if necessary. The Council accepted that the Federation's intentions were peaceful, but what of the future? There had been mention of a hostile Klingon Empire . . .

Kirk would have liked to have stayed to argue the question further, but he had already received word from Spock that an ion storm of considerable violence was beginning to blow through the Halkan system—and in fact Kirk could already see evidence of it in the Halkan weather, which was becoming decidedly lowering. To stay longer might risk disruption of transporter transmission, which would strand the landing party for an unknown time. In addition, it was Spock's opinion that the heart of the magnetic storm represented a danger to the *Enterprise* herself.

On this kind of opinion, Kirk would not have argued with Spock for a second; the First Officer never erred by a hairline on the wrong side of conservatism. Kirk ordered the landing party beamed up.

That hairline was very nearly split, this time. On the first attempt, the transporter got the party only partly materialized aboard ship when the beam suffered a phase reversal and all four of them found themselves standing on a bare plateau on the Halkan planet, illuminated only by a barrage of lightning. It was nearly five minutes later before the familiar Transporter Room sprang fully into being around them.

Kirk stepped quickly from the platform toward Spock. "We may or may not get those power crystals . . ."

And then he stopped, in midstep as well as midsentence. For Spock and the transporter chief were saluting, and a most peculiar salute it was: the arms first folded loosely, then raised stiffly horizontal and squared out. Their uniforms were different, too; basically, they were the same as before, but they were much altered in detail, and the detail had a savage military flair—broad belts bearing exposed phasers and what seemed to be ceremonial daggers, shoulder boards, braid. And the Federation breast symbol was gone; instead, there was a blazon which looked like a galaxy with a dagger through it. A similar symbol, in brilliant color, was on one wall of the room, and the equipment was all in the wrong places—indeed, a few pieces of it were completely unfamiliar.

But what struck Kirk most of all was the change in Spock. Vulcans all look somewhat satanic to Earthmen encountering them for the first time, but it had been many years since Kirk had thoroughly gotten over this impression of his First Officer. Now it was back, full force. Spock looked cold, hard, almost fanatical.

Kirk dropped his hands to his belt—since he did not know how to return the strange salute—and encountered something else unfamiliar. A brief glance confirmed what he had feared: his uniform, too, had undergone the strange changes.

"At norm," Spock said to the transporter chief, in a voice loaded with savage harshness. "Captain, do you mean the Halkans have weapons that could resist us? Our socioanalysis indicates that they are incapable of violence."

Kirk could not answer. He was spared having to, for at

that moment Sulu entered the Transporter Room. His movements, his manner, were cold, arrogant, hypercompetent, but that was not the worst of it. The symbol on his breast, the galaxy with the dagger through it, had inside it also a clenched fist, around the blade of the dagger, from which blood was dripping. It was an extreme parody of something familiar; it showed that the gentle Sulu, the ship's navigator and helmsman, was now her chief security officer.

Sulu did not salute. He barked, "Status of mission, Captain?"

"No change," Kirk said carefully.

"Standard procedure, then?"

Kirk did not know what this question meant under these eerie circumstances, but he doubted that operating by the book—whatever the book might say—would accomplish much more than delaying matters, and time was what he needed. Therefore, he nodded.

Sulu turned to the nearest intercom. "Mr. Chekov. You will program phaser barrage on Halkan cities, at the rate of one million electron volts per day, in a gradually contracting circle around each. Report when ready."

"Right, Mr. Sulu." Was Kirk imagining it, or was there something thick and gloating in Chekov's voice?

"Unfortunate," Spock said, "that this race should choose suicide to annexation. They possess qualities that could be useful to the Empire."

There was the sputtering hum of an overload from the transporter. Spock's head jerked toward the transporter chief, and then, slowly, inexorably, he advanced on the man. Incredibly, the transporter chief *cringed*.

"Are you not aware, chief, that we are in a magnetic storm? And that you were ordered to compensate?"

"Mr. Spock, sir, I'm sorry. The ion-flux is so unpredictable . . ."

"Carelessness with Empire equipment is intolerable." Spock held out his hand toward Sulu, without looking. "Mr. Sulu, your agonizer."

Sulu plucked a small device from his belt and dropped it in Spock's outstretched palm. In a vicious burlesque of the Vulcan neck pinch, Spock clapped it to the transporter chief's shoulder.

The man screamed. Spock prolonged the agony. When he let go, the chief dropped writhing to the deck.

"More attention to duty next time, please. Mr. Scott, the storm has produced minor damage in your section. Doctor McCoy, there are also some minor injuries requiring your attention." Abruptly, he kicked the semiconscious man on the floor. "You might begin with this hulk."

McCoy, whose running feud with the First Officer had always had a solid undercurrent of affection to moderate it, wore the look of a man whose worst nightmare has abruptly come true. Kirk saw him balling his fists, and moved in fast.

"Get moving, Dr. McCoy. You too, Mr. Scott."

Their expressions flickered for a moment, and then both looked down. Now they knew how the Captain wanted them to play it. At least, Kirk hoped so. In any event, they went out without further comment.

The transporter chief dragged himself to his feet to follow. It did not seem to surprise him at all that the ship's doctor, who had just been ordered to attend to him, had not said a word to him. He said, "Mr. Spock . . ."

"What?"

"Sir, the beam power jumped for a moment, sir—just as the landing party materialized. I never saw anything like it before. I thought you ought to know, sir."

Kirk had already heard more 'sirs' in ten minutes than were normal to the *Enterprise* in a week. Spock said, "Another inefficiency?"

"No, sir, the settings were perfectly normal. I made my error after the party arrived, sir, if I may so remind you."

"Very well. Go to Sickbay. Captain, do you feel any ill effects?"

Kirk could answer that one with no trouble. "Yes, Mr. Spock, I am decidedly shaken up. I expect Lieutenant Uhura is too. I believe we too had better report to Sickbay for a checkup."

"You will of course report instantly if you are found incompetent to command," Sulu said. It was not a question.

"Of course, Mr. Sulu."

"And the matter of the Halkans? A quick bombardment would solve the problem with the least effort."

"I am aware of your—orders—Mr. Sulu. I will give you my judgment as soon as I—feel myself assured that I am competent to give it."

"Most sensible."

As Kirk and Uhura left, everyone again saluted—except Sulu. On the trip to Sickbay, Kirk became aware that there were more guards posted along the corridors than he had ever seen except during the worst kind of major alert. None of them were in standard uniforms; instead, they wore fatigues, like civilian workmen. All saluted. None seemed surprised not to have the salutes returned.

Uhura gasped with relief as the door of Sickbay slid closed behind them and the four people who had been the landing party were once more alone together. "What's *happened?*" she said in a low, intense voice.

"Don't talk too fast," Kirk said instantly, though he himself was talking as fast as he could possibly get the words out. He stabbed a finger toward McCoy's intercom. "Something in the air suggests that that thing is permanently open."

The rest nodded. It was a lucky thing that they had all been together so long; it made elliptical talk possible among them. "Now, Bones, that medical. I want you to check for likely effects. I suggest brainwaves first."

"I've already checked myself and Scotty, sir. No hallucinatory or hypnotic effects. We are dealing with—uh, a perception of reality, if you follow me."

"I'm afraid I do. Mr. Scott, do you detect any changes in the *Enterprise* which—might have a bearing on our reactions?"

Scott inclined his head and listened. "I hear some sort of difference in the impulse engines. Of course they may just be laboring against the magnetic storm. However, the difference seems to me to be, well, technological in nature, sir."

"Excuse me, Captain," Uhura said, "but I feel a little out of my depth. I felt quite dizzy for a moment after we materialized in the beams. Would it be possible . . ."

She did not finish the sentence, but instead made the gesture of someone fitting a bucket or a large hat over McCoy's intercom. The physician's eyebrows went up. He stepped to where his diagnostic apparatus should have been, veered in disgust as he found that it had been moved, and then flicked switches.

"I should have thought of that in the first place," he said, "but I'm as confused as anybody here. Everybody used to complain that my stereotaxic screen jammed the intercoms; let's hope it still does."

"We'll have to take the chance," Kirk said. "Lieutenant Uhura, I felt the same effect. At the same time, we were in our normal Transporter Room—and then it faded, we were back on the planet, and then got beamed back to this situation—whatever it is. And the transporter chief—where is he, by the way?"

"I made him mildly sick," McCoy said, "and sent him to quarters. A nasty reversal of role for a doctor, but I want him out of Spock's reach for a while."

"Well, he mentioned an abnormal effect in the transporter itself. And there's this ion storm."

"Captain," Scott said slowly, "are we thinking the same thing?"

"I don't know, Scotty. But everything fits thus far. It fits with a parallel universe, coexisting with ours, on another dimensional plane—or maybe on another level of probability; everything duplicated—almost. An Empire instead of a Federation. Another *Enterprise*—another Spock . . ."

"Another Jim Kirk?" Scott said quietly. "Another Dr. McCoy?"

"No," McCoy said in startled realization. "An exchange! If *we're here* . . ."

"Our counterparts were beaming at the same time," Kirk said. "Ion storms are common enough, after all. Another storm disrupted another set of circuits. Now we're here; they're on *our* ship, and probably asking each other much the same questions. And coming to the same tentative conclusions. They'll ask the computer what to do. That's what we'll have to do."

McCoy began to pace. "What about the Halkans? We can't let them be wiped out, even if this is another, completely different set of Halkans, in another universe."

"I don't know, Bones. I've got to buy a lot of time. Scotty, get below and short the main phaser coupling.

Make it look like the storm blew the standby circuits. Lieutenant Uhura, get to your post and run today's communications from Starfleet Command, or whatever the equivalent is here. I've got to know my exact orders, and options, if any. And by the way, when we want to talk to each other after we're separated, use communicators, and on the subspace band only. And scramble, too."

Uhura and the engineer nodded and left. McCoy had halted his pacing before a sort of glass cage. In it was what appeared to be a large bird, affixed with electrodes. A chart hung beside it.

"What in blazes!" McCoy said. "Jim, look at this. A specimen of an 'annexed' race. I.Q., 180. Experiment in life-support for humans under conditions prevailing on its native planet—heart and lung modifications. It's alive—and if I'm any judge, it's in agony. I won't have such an abomination in my Sickbay!"

"You'll have to, for a while," Kirk said, not without sympathy. "We've got to stay in character until we can get more information. It's an ugly universe, and we don't want to do anything that'll get us stuck with it."

On the bridge, there was a huge duplicate of the galaxy-and-dagger device, and the Captain's chair had widely flared arms, almost like a throne. The man who should be Chekov was eyeing Uhura with open, deliberate, speculative interest, his intent unmistakable. Nobody else seemed to find this unusual or even interesting. Kirk went directly to her.

"Any new orders, Lieutenant?"

"No, sir. You are still ordered to annihilate the Halkans, unless they comply. No alternative action has been prescribed."

"Thank you." He went to his chair and sank in. It felt downright luxurious. "Report, Mr. Sulu?"

"Phasers locked on Target A, Captain. Approaching optimum range. Shall I commence fire?"

"I want a status report first." He touched the intercom. "Mr. Scott?"

"Scott here, sir. I have no change to report, sir. No damage to phasers."

72

"Very good, Mr. Scott." In fact it was very bad, but there was no help for it. As he switched out, Spock came onto the bridge.

"The planet's rotation is carrying the primary target beyond arc of phaser lock," Sulu said. "Shall I correct orbit to new firing position?"

"No."

Sulu flicked a switch. "Now locked on secondary target city."

"Mr. Spock," Kirk said. "You said the Halkans could be useful. After my visit with them, I agree."

"If they chose to cooperate. They have not."

"Lieutenant Uhura, contact the Halkan Council. We'll make one more try." Noting Spock's surprise, he added, "This is a new race. They offer other things of value besides dilithium crystals."

"But—it is clear that we cannot expect cooperation. They have refused the Empire. Command Procedure dictates that we provide the customary example. A serious breach of Standard Orders . . ."

"I have my reasons, Mr. Spock—and I'll make them clear in my own good time."

"Captain," Uhura said, "the Halkan leader is waiting on Channel B."

Kirk swung to the small viewscreen above Uhura's station. Tharn was on the screen. He looked much tireder, indeed more tragic, than he had when Kirk had seen him last. Now, how would it be possible to make this sound plausible?

"It is useless to resist us," he said at random.

"We do not resist you," Tharn said.

"You have, uh, twelve hours in which to reconsider your position."

"Twelve years, Captain Kirk, or twelve thousand, will make no difference," Tharn said calmly and with great dignity. "We are ethically compelled to refuse your demand for dilithium crystals. You would use their power to destroy."

"We will level your planet and take what we want. *That* is destruction. You would die as a race . . ."

"To preserve what we are. Yes. Perhaps someday your

73

slave planets will all defy you, as we have done. When that comes, how will your starships be able to control a whole galaxy?"

"Switch out, Lieutenant." The screen went blank.

"Twelve hours, Captain?" Spock said. "That is unprecedented."

"Phasers off, Mr. Sulu."

"This conduct must be reported, Captain," Spock said. "You have placed yourself in a most grave position."

"You are at liberty to do so, Mr. Spock," Kirk said, rising. "Take charge. I will be in the briefing room. Inform me of any change. Lieutenant Uhura, attend me there and order Dr. McCoy and Mr. Scott also to report there. Mr. Chekov, relieve Lieutenant Uhura."

He could only hope that this flurry of orders, plus his breach of an unknown regulation, would obscure the fact that he had just called together the landing party.

"Everybody watch your step," Scott said. "They move up through assassination around here. My engine-room chief just tried for me—not personally, but through henchmen. I only got out of it because one of them switched sides."

"What about the technology, Scotty?"

"Mostly variations in instrumentation. Nothing I can't handle. As for star-readings—everything's where it ought to be—except us."

Kirk crossed to the desk and looked down at the computer tap. "Let's see what we're up against. Computer, this is the Captain. Record a Security Research, to be classified under my voiceprint and Mr. Scott's."

"Recorded," said the computer in a harsh masculine voice. Evidently this universe had never discovered that men pay more attention to a machine when its voice is feminine.

"Produce all data relevant to recent magnetic storm, and correlate following hypothesis. Could a storm of that magnitude cause a power surge in transporter circuits, creating momentary interdimensional contact with a parallel universe?"

"Affirmative."

"At such a moment, could persons in each universe, in

74

he act of beaming, be transposed with their counterparts
n the other universe?"

"Affirmative."

"Can conditions necessary to such an event be artificial-
ly reproduced?"

"Affirmative."

"Record procedure and switch off."

A slot in the desk opened and a spool of tape slid out.
Kirk handed it to Scott. "It looks like the ball is yours,
Scotty."

"I'll have to tap the power for it out of the warp
engines, and balance it for the four of us," the engineer
said dubiously. "It's a two-man job, and I'm afraid you'd
be too conspicuous, Captain. So would Lieutenant Uhura.
Come on, McCoy, let's lay it out."

"I'm not an engineer," McCoy said indignantly.

"You will be. Captain, keep up our public relations,
please!"

The two went out. After a moment, Uhura said, "Captain—the way this ship is run—what kind of people *are*
we in this universe? I mean, what kind of people do we
have to pretend to be?"

"Let's find out. Computer. Readout of official record of
current command."

"Captain: James T. Kirk. Succeeded to command *E. S.
S. Enterprise* through assassination of Captain Karl Franz.
First action: suppression of Gorlan uprising, through destruction of rebel home planet. Second action: execution of
five thousand colonists on S Doradus Nine, forcing colony
to retract secession. Third action . . ."

"Cancel. Lieutenant, do you really want to hear it tell
you what *you're* like?"

Lt. Uhura shuddered. "No. If the way the local Chekov
looks at me is any clue, I'll probably hear that my prede-
cessor at my post was my lover, and I got the job by
knifing him. How can you run a fifty billion credit starship like a pirate vessel?"

"Pirate ships were pretty efficiently run, Lieutenant.
Every man feared those above him—with the strongest at
the top. Morgan took Panama with his buccaneer ships as
neatly as a squadron of naval vessels might have."

"And then was stabbed in his sleep?"

"No, henchmen protected him—not out of respect or devotion, but because his abilities brought them what they wanted. Other checks and balances—other means to the same end."

"But what end?"

"This ship is efficient—or it wouldn't exist. Its Captain was efficient, or he'd be dead. And this Empire will get the dilithium crystals it wants—efficiently."

Uhura's expression remained grim. "And what do you suppose our counterparts are doing, aboard *our* version of the *Enterprise*?"

"I hope they're faking as well as or better than we are. Otherwise, when we get back, we'll all be up on charges." The intercom beeped. "Kirk here."

"Sir, I'm having trouble on this line, I can barely hear you."

"Right." Kirk switched off, produced his communicator, and set it to subspace level and on "scramble." "Okay, Scotty, here I am. Go ahead."

"We can do it, Captain. But when we interrupt engine circuits, to tie in the power increase to the transporters, it'll show up on the Security Board. We'll just need a second, but . . ."

"All right, wait a minute." Kirk thought fast. "Lieutenant Uhura, this is going to be nasty. I noticed the local Chekov giving you the eye . . ."

"He made a flat-out pass at me before you came on the bridge, Captain."

"All the better. For the sake of our getting home, could you encourage him a little?"

Uhura said slowly, "I wouldn't pull a mean trick like that on *our* Chekov. And this one gives me the crawls. But—of course, Captain, if you wish."

"Good girl. Scotty, Uhura can create a diversion on the bridge, which will draw Sulu's attention, I think, at your signal. Now, everyone back to posts, before somebody cottons to the fact that this looks like a council of war."

Uhura slipped out silently. Kirk, too, was about to go, when Spock entered the briefing room by another door, and saluted.

"Captain, a word with you, if I may."

"Of course."

"I should regret your death."

Kirk raised his eyebrows. "Very kind of you, Mr. pock."

"Kindness is not involved. As you know, I do not esire the captaincy. I much prefer my scientific duties— nd I am frankly content to be a lesser target."

"Quite logical, as always, Mr. Spock."

"Therefore I am moved to inquire if you intend to ersist in your unusual course of action regarding the Halkans."

"My orders stand."

"I presume you have a plan. I have found you to be an xcellent officer. Our missions together have been success- ul ones."

"I remember," Kirk said. "Perhaps better than you do."

"I never forget anything."

"I remember that too. Then you will also remember the llogic of waste, Mr. Spock. Is it logical to destroy poten- ial workers—equipment—valuable installations—without making every effort to put them on a useful basis? Surely he Empire can afford a little patience."

"Logically, we must maintain the terror," Spock said. "Otherwise the Empire will develop soft spots, and the rot vill spread."

"The Halkans made the same point. Is history with us? Conquest is easy—control is not."

"History seldom repeats itself," Spock said, frowning. "Yet I concede that no regime such as ours has ever survived the eventual fury of its victims. The question is, has our power become so vast, quantitatively, as to make a *qualitative* change in that situation? Space, as you say, is against us; its sheer vastness makes communication diffi- cult, let alone control—I did not know you were a phil- osopher, Captain. We have never talked this way before."

"Perhaps overdue, Mr. Spock."

"That is more than possible. I do not judge Command- er Moreau to be much of a thinker."

There was quite a long silence, during which Kirk won- dered who in blazes Commander Moreau was. Most like- ly, the man who *was* gunning for the Captain's job.

"Sir," Spock said finally, "I have received a private

message from Starfleet Command. I am committing a serious breach of regulations by informing you of its contents. But other considerations supervene. Briefly, I have been instructed to wait until planet dawn over principal target, to permit you to complete our mission. Your delaying maneuver was of course reported to Starfleet Command by Mr. Sulu."

"And if I don't?"

"In that event," Spock said, his voice somehow both harsh and reluctant at the same time, "I am ordered to have you killed, and proceed against the Halkans, as the new Captain of the *Enterprise*. I shall of course remove Moreau too, making it appear that he was killed by *your* agents."

"Logical," Kirk said bitterly. "But thank you for the warning, Mr. Spock."

"I regret the situation. I shall remain in my quarters throughout the night—in case you should wish to contact me privately."

"Thank you again. But there will be no change."

"Sir—under the circumstances—may I express the greatest curiosity concerning your motives?"

"I'm almost tempted to tell you, Mr. Spock. But you'll understand in time. Carry on."

When he left, Kirk sat down at the table. He knew he should be back on the bridge, carrying on the masquerade. But even with Spock's odd sort of cooperation, even supposing Scotty could get them back to their own universe, that would leave the biggest problem unsolved: the fate of the Halkans in this alternate universe. No matter what happened to Kirk, McCoy, Scott and Uhura, the Halkans seemed to be destined for slaughter. And he could think of no way to prevent it.

Then the communicator beeped. "Kirk here."

"Captain, this is Scotty. I've got the whole thing rigged, with McCoy's help. I'm thinking of making him assistant engineer. But in checking it out with the computer, I discovered somethin' vurra worrisome. The two-way matter transmission affected local field density between the two universes—and it's increasing. We've got to move fast. We have half an hour at most. If we miss, we couldn't push back through for a century."

"What's the procedure, Scotty?"

"We're about ready to bridge power from the warp engines to the beams. You've got to go to the main controls and free the board, so we can lock in. Give us ten clock minutes, then you and Lieutenant Uhura create your diversion, and run like Martian scopolamanders for the Transporter Room."

"Right. Count down on the time. Five . . . four . . . three . . . two . . . one . . . *hack*."

"Got you. Good luck, Captain."

No time now to worry about the Halkans; but Kirk worried, nonetheless. On the bridge, Sulu looked speculatively, coldly, at Kirk as Kirk resumed the Captain's chair.

"Orders, Captain?"

"Prepare to lock on to Target A. We fire at planet dawn."

Sulu smiled coldly. "I am glad to see that you have come to your senses. All this computer activity obviously has produced no alternative answer, except to make me wonder if you had gone soft. And while Mr. Spock would no doubt make an excellent captain, you were once clearly the better one. I hope you will continue to be."

Kirk was so sick at the order he had had to give that he did not bother to disguise his disgust. "You don't miss much, do you, Mr. Sulu."

"A good Security Officer misses nothing. Otherwise he would deserve to go to the Agony Booth."

*Well,* Kirk thought grimly, *you may yet, Mr. Pseudo-Sulu. Obviously you don't know what that computer activity really was about.*

The Halkan planet's image was showing on Uhura's viewscreen. Chekov was watching her, with very much the same lubricious expression as before. She looked up at the image, and then, as if to herself, said, "Just once, I'd like to think about something besides death."

Sulu shot one contemptuous glance at her and went back to watching the master board. When Scott made his power switch from the warp engines to the transporters, he would catch it.

Uhura looked away from the screen toward Chekov.

Her glance was steady for a moment, and then she looked down. Her veiled eyes suggested that she just might be persuaded to change her mind.

The navigator grinned, leaned back in his seat. His arm went out and around toward Uhura's waist.

Sulu paid no attention. And there was one minute left.

*Slap!*

Sulu looked up. Uhura was standing, in furious indignation. She fell back, one, two, three calculated steps toward Sulu's board. Chekov, astonishment changing to rage, was standing too.

But Sulu seemed to be no more than amused. "As you were, Chekov."

Chekov was not ready to be as he was. He seemed almost ready to attack Uhura. Kirk saw an opening and jumped in.

"Is this the kind of horseplay that goes on when I'm not on the bridge? And at moments as critical as this? Mr. Chekov, you are on report; I'll tend to you later. Lieutenant Uhura, you provoked this; proceed immediately to the Booth. Mr. Sulu, take Lieutenant Uhura's post."

"Sir," Sulu said. "Why are you also leaving?" The 'sir' was silkily insulting.

"I am going to explain personally to Lieutenant Uhura why she is in the Booth. I'll return shortly; in the meantime, follow standard procedure."

He had caught the streak of sadism and lechery in these loathsome counterparts of his crew. Every man on the bridge grinned slyly and licked his lips.

Then Kirk and Uhura were out, and running for the Transporter Room.

Spock and two crewmen were waiting for them there, with drawn phasers.

"Well, Mr. Spock? Have you decided to kill me now, even though I am following my orders?"

"No, Captain. But strange things have occurred since the return of your landing party—including some remarkable calls upon the computer, which I find sealed against me. Nothing in the computer should be sealed against the First Officer. And you are preparing to use an enormous surge of power in the transporter. That could be most dangerous. I must ask you: where do you think you are going, Captain—you and your three conspirators?"

"Home," Kirk said.

"To the alternate universe?"

"You understand *that?*"

"Yes, Captain. And I concur. I will ask you only to gun me down with a stun charge before you leave. My henchmen here will support any story I tell thereafter."

McCoy said, "Mr. Spock, in my universe you and I often disagreed, and in this universe I hated you. But you seem to be a man of integrity in both universes."

"It is only logical," Spock said. "You must return to your universe, so that I can have *my* Captain back. I will operate the transporter. You have two minutes and twenty seconds left."

"Mr. Spock," Kirk said. "I will shave that time as close as possible. I want to ask you this: How long do you think it will be before the Halkans' prediction of galactic revolt is realized?"

Spock blinked, as if the sudden change of subject had taken him unawares. "I would estimate—approximately two hundred and forty years."

"And what will be the inevitable outcome?"

"The Empire will be overthrown, of course. A sort of federation may replace it, if the period of interdestruction is not too devastating."

"Mr. Spock. Consider the illogic of waste. Waste of lives, resources, potentials, time. It is not logical of you to give your vast talents to an empire which you know is doomed."

"You have one minute and twenty-three seconds."

"When change is both predictable and beneficial, why do you resist it?"

"Suicide is also illogical. One man cannot summon the future."

Kirk closed on this man, who looked and acted so much like his First Officer, and yet had so little of the real Spock's hidden humanity in him. "Mr. Spock, one man can change the present. *Be* the Captain of this *Enterprise,* whether you want the job or not. Find a logical reason for sparing the Halkans, and making it stick. Push where it gives. You can defend yourself better than any man in the fleet, if you are anything like *my* First Officer, and I think you are. In every revolution, there's one man with a vision. Which will it be? Past or future? Tyranny, or the right to hope, trust, love? Even here, Spock, you cannot be totally without the decency you've shown on the—the other side. Use it, make it work!"

"You must go," Spock said. "But my Captain never said any such words to me. I will remember them. I can promise nothing else, though I will save the Halkans if I can. Now, quickly! You have eighteen seconds left! Shoot! And goodbye, Jim Kirk."

Kirk stepped onto the transporter platform with the others. He raised the phaser, set to "stun," but it was very hard to pull the trigger all the same.

Kirk relaxed in his chair, soaking in normality. Nearby, Uhura was giving poor Chekov a look that dripped icicles. Kirk himself still felt a little uncomfortable to find Sulu— the 'real' Sulu—at his elbow.

McCoy, however, evidently had not found it at all hard to readjust; his vast knowledge of psychology under stress also enabled him to understand himself. He said enthusiastically to Spock, "When I came out of the beams, Spocko boy, I was so pleased to see you that I almost kissed you. Luckily, revulsion at the very notion set in two seconds later."

"I am grateful that it did," Spock said.

"Mr. Spock," Kirk said, "Scotty tells me that had you not detected our counterparts immediately, restrained and questioned them, duplicated our calculations, and above all had them shoved into the transporter chamber all ready to make the exchange at the one precise moment, we'd have been stranded forever. I salute you; you have come through for the umpteenth time. But—how did you do it?"

"Sir," Spock said, "you know me as well as any man. But there are elements in my own heart that I do not show very readily. I had to call on them."

"Don't explain if you don't want to. But it would be useful to know how you managed it."

Spock raised his head and looked at some spot faraway in space.

"A civilized man," he said at last, "can easily play the part of a barbarian, as you all did in the other universe. He has only to look into his own soul for the remnants of the savage ancestors from which he sprang, and then—revert. But your counterparts, when we beamed them aboard, were savages to begin with—and had no core of civilization or humanity to which they could revert. The contrast was rather striking."

McCoy said, "Spock, could *you* have played the savage, if you'd been switched along with the rest of us?"

Very seriously, Spock said, "Dr. McCoy, I *am* a savage. Both here, and there. But some day, I hope to outgrow it."

# FRIDAY'S CHILD

## (D. C. Fontana)

Monday's child is fair of face.
Tuesday's child is full of grace.
Wednesday's child is loving and giving.
Thursday's child works hard for a living.
Friday's child is full of woe.
But the child that is born on the Sabbath Day
Is brave and bonny and good and gay.
(Harper's Weekly, 1887)

Even had Kirk not already known that Teer Akaar was
High Chief of the ten tribes of Ceres, it would have been
plain from the moment that he, Spock and McCoy materialized before the encampment that the Akaars were persons of consequence. Before each of the tents—which
were on the edge of a brushy area—stood a pole bearing a
family banner, and each of these was surmounted by
another flag emblazoned with Akaar's tribal emblem, a
flight of abstract birds.

A few tribesmen and women, wearing vividly colored
robes cut in simple tunic style, stared in astonishment as
the three from the *Enterprise* shimmered into existence
out of nothing, and then silently ducked away into their
own tents as another man stepped into view from the
largest pavilion. This man's tunic was plain black, with
the distinctive bird design embroidered on the shoulder. He
seemed to be about forty-five, reed slim, tough as a leather
quirt. Looking straight at Kirk, he put his right fist over
his heart and then extended the hand out before him,

palm up. The gesture was easy to read: *My heart and all that I own are open to you.*

"I am Maab, of the House of Akaar," he said. "Our tents are honored."

"You honor us," Kirk said. Thinking fast, he made a half-bow with both hands out before him, palms up, and then drew the hands to his chest. *Your hospitality is accepted with open heart.* It might not have been the right answer, but it seemed to do.

"The High Chief awaits your coming," Maab said, gesturing toward the tent and then leading the way. They an increase in the number of 'incidents' in the past month. friendly toward the Federation, but Klingon ships had been reported in this sector, and though technically the Federation and the Empire were at peace, there had been an increase in the number of incidents in the past month. It was vital that the mission to Ceres not become an incident.

There were two men, as well as a woman, inside the tent, but Maab's full, deep bow of total subservience instantly made evident which man was Teer Akaar, a tall, broad-shouldered man in his late fifties, in a white robe with black birds. The ritual gestures were exchanged, and introductions made all around. Maab, it developed, was Teer Akaar's brother. The tall man in his late teens was Raal, the chief's son; and the kneeling young woman, who was quite lovely, was the chief's wife Eleen ("My second wife, and an honor to my house"). As Raal helped her to rise, it became clear that she was pregnant.

"Come," Akaar said, gesturing toward a table so low that it almost scraped the carpets. "I wish to hear your words about the rocks of the mountains."

Kirk motioned to Spock, who set upon the table several pieces of raw stone and the many-paged, pre-prepared formal agreement. They all sat down on cushions, except the woman, who retired to a curtained-off area, and Raal, who quietly left through the front entrance. It was getting dark outside.

"A geological survey," Kirk said, "has revealed that your world has valuable deposits of a mineral called topaline. I have been authorized to negotiate for Federation mining rights for this mineral."

85

"My people are herders and tradesmen, Captain," Akaar said. "We do not understand how a rock may be of value."

"You make your weapons of iron. You often trade in gold and silver."

"Iron has long been known to our weapons makers. Gold and silver came with Federation trade ships—they have little meaning to us. But they are metal, not rock such as this." He nudged the chunk of topaline ore.

"Chief Akaar, I trust you will bear with me for a long explanation. The Federation has hundreds of colonies which are mining operations, and research projects, on planets and asteroids that normally could not maintain our life forms. As your own legends hint, you yourselves are descendants of an Earth colony. Those colonists named your planet after an asteroid in Earth's own solar system, a five-hundred-mile ball of rock that was the first asteroid to be colonized—though it hasn't even an atmosphere."

"Then how is this done?" Akaar said.

"We create artificial domes under which we maintain air we can breathe," Spock said. "Topaline contains minute quantities of a metal which is essential to such life-support systems. Not only is it rare, but it must be constantly replaced."

"Why?" Maab said. "Does it rust, or wear out?"

Spock was obviously starting to explain, but Kirk held up his hand. These people had utterly forgotten the technology which had brought them to this planet, centuries ago. Nothing short of a cram course in physics would make clear to them the concept of radioactive half-life.

"Something like that," Kirk said. "And the fact that there is so little of it even in topaline means that the ore has to be transported in bulk to special refining plants."

"Then clearly it is of enormous value," Maab said. "What then do you offer for it?"

"An honest price," Kirk said, "in whatever medium of exchange you favor."

Maab leaned forward. Suddenly, he looked angry. "You Earthmen," he said harshly, "come hiding your lies behind papers of promise. Then you steal . . ."

Akaar slammed a hand flat on the table top. "Maab!"

"They have cheated others," Maab said, staring hard at his brother. "We have heard. They have no honor . . ."

"You will be silent!"

"Nay, I will not. We are not of one mind on this. There are many who do not wish this treaty."

"Leave us. You cannot speak for the tribes."

Maab arose. "I will leave. But many are not as gullible as our High Chief. We will be heard."

He turned and strode out furiously, leaving behind a thick, heavy silence. Finally, Akaar stirred uncomfortably and said, "My brother dishonors me. Yet it may be said that your history gives him some reason to distrust you."

"Our ancient history, perhaps," Kirk said. "And perhaps dimly and inaccurately recalled."

"Certainly you have done us no wrong. But Maab has heard of other places and other peoples. He uses these to speak against you."

"How has he heard such stories?"

"By truth, I do not know," Akaar said. "Earth traders, perhaps. A few come for the wool of our *zakdirs*."

"Then these are mere rumors, at best," Kirk said. "Our treaties are faithfully upheld."

"I take your word, Captain. I understand the things in this paper, and I will give it to the council of tribes this night. In the meantime, I bid you hang your weapons in my tent while you eat, and then rejoin us."

Kirk had known this was coming, for Spock had earlier made a most thorough study of the culture. But there was nothing that could be done about it. At a clap of Akaar's hands, a tribesman appeared, and the three men from the *Enterprise* handed over their phasers to him, and also their communicators, for to these herdsmen any machine seemed likely to be a weapon—especially if its custody was refused.

"I accept the guardianship of these weapons," Akaar said with singsong formality, "as an earnest of long peace between us. Keel, you will show these visitors to their tent, and have food brought them."

The meal was strange, but sumptuous, and served by a most scantily-clad Cerean girl of whom it was impossible not to be aware. Trying not to look pointedly the other way, McCoy said, "But I thought topaline deposits on Altimara would be sufficient for another two years."

"Altimara was a disappointment," Kirk said. "The two most promising veins petered out. They'll be able to maintain full supply for all colonies for six months. By then, the mining project here has to be in full operation."

"No reserves?"

Spock said, "There is a convoy of freighters on its way now from refineries on Lorigan to the colonies in this quadrant. But it will be the last; Lorigan has been shut down. Exhausted."

"Umph," McCoy said. "These endless mineralogical assignments are dull work. And Jim, this argument between Akaar and Maab—I don't like the feel of it."

"Nor I. But it's not our quarrel. We have to abide by the Council's ruling. Clearly Maab will have a strong voice in it. If he wins, well, maybe he has a price of his own."

"You'd deal with him?" McCoy said.

"I'm authorized to deal with whoever can give this planet's mining rights to the Federation," Kirk said quietly. "I am *not* authorized to take sides in any local struggle for power, Bones."

"In that connection," Spock said, picking up a slice of some pink fruit and eyeing it as if it were an unusually uninteresting insect, "I found it odd to see that two guards were placed in front of the High Chief's tent as soon as Keel led us away from it. In addition to the usual swords and knives, these carried the boomerang-like instrument these people call the *klugat*. Such an arsenal makes me wonder whether the guards were posted to defend Teer Akaar from attack—or from escaping."

Outside the tent there was a sudden shout, then another, and then the unmistakable clash of metal on metal.

"I think we're about to find out," Kirk said, springing up. All three dashed for the entrance.

They were met outside by three tribesmen, whose swords were instantly at their throats. The encampment was a bedlam. Akaar was in the center of a swirl of combat, defending himself like a hawk at bay. He was not alone, but his party was clearly outnumbered. His son was already dead. In the light of the campfire, Kirk could see that Maab was directing the attackers, and also prominent among them was Keel.

A *klugat* struck Akaar. He staggered, wounded in the side, blood flooding the side of his tunic. He had only two defenders left.

"Jim! We can't just . . ."

"Stand fast, Bones," Kirk said in an iron voice.

Akaar tried for his brother with one last thrust of his sword. Maab sidestepped it easily, and Akaar fell. His two last defenders, though apparently not seriously hurt, fell with him, kneeling before Maab in servile supplication.

The guards around Kirk's party prodded them forward. Maab waved Keel and another tribesman into what had been Akaar's pavilion. Then he smiled slightly at Kirk.

"You were wise not to try to interfere, Captain. This is none of your concern."

"We would have interfered if we could. We don't approve of murder."

"There has been no murder," Maab said stiffly. "We gave my brother an honorable death. This is revolution."

"I'm not interested in what you call it. However, you are not the man into whose custody we gave our equipment. I want it returned."

Maab's answer was predictable, but he did not have to give it, for at this moment Eleen stumbled out of the tent, herded at sword point by Keel and his fellow assassin. She was already frightened, but her fright became terror as she saw Akaar's body. Maab tripped her and simultaneously shoved her with the flat of his sword, so that she fell partly into the still red ashes of the campfire.

She screamed, half with pain and half with the doom of Maab's sword raised above her. Moving like lightning, Kirk slammed Maab aside, at the same time twisting his wrist in one of the very few directions the human wrist is not built to go; the sword fell. McCoy, only half a step behind, knelt beside Eleen; and with a smooth gesture, Spock scooped up the fallen sword.

Vulcans are tightly rational creatures, but in background they are a warrior race. Spock with a sword in his hand was a sight to give even a Cerean pause. They closed in with exaggerated caution.

And then, as McCoy lifted Eleen gently to examine her burned arm, all the Cereans gasped—and the woman herself, with an expression of loathing impossible to misinterpret, jerked herself free of the doctor's support.

"What's the matter with you, woman?" McCoy said sharply. "None of that, now. I'm only trying to help."

"And you have brought death upon yourself," Maab said slowly. "I would have let you go. But now . . ."

"You talk nonsense," Kirk said. "Killing an armed man who has a chance to defend himself is one thing. Murdering a defenseless woman is something else. She can't hurt you. You have the Chieftanship—you don't need her life."

"It is you who talk nonsense. Raal is dead, but this child that is to come is also of Akaar and still lives. It too must die before I may become chief—cleanly, by the sword. Moreover, Captain, by our law, only a husband may lay hands on his wife; for any other man, the penalty is death. I have not touched Eleen, nor would I have; but this your officer . . ."

"We're not governed by your law. Any charges against us will have to be brought before Starfleet Command, which will weigh them on their merits, one set of laws against the other."

"We know who would lose that judgment," Maab said. "On our world, our laws, and only our laws, prevail."

"Our ship will send a landing party to investigate our silence," Spock said, leveling the captured sword at the bridge of Maab's nose.

Maab did not flinch. "I think not," he said, with an odd, lopsided smile. "I think they will be too busy."

Kirk and Spock shot a swift glance at each other. Each knew precisely what the other was thinking. With that single, irresistible, and absolutely unnecessary brag, Maab had let slip the fact that there was more to this situation than simple tribal politics—a *lot* more.

Now had to come the hardest game of all: waiting in patience, even to the verge of death, to find out what it was.

In the guest tent, which was now their jail, Kirk, Spock and McCoy sat around the table where once they had been fed so sumptuously. Now two assassins were on guard inside the tent entrance. Eleen sat as far away from them all as she could, a light cloak over her tunic, but even more markedly huddled behind a wall of self-imposed isolation. Her arm had still not been tended; she had refused, and now she was refusing also to show any pain.

McCoy leaned his elbows on the table and looked unhappily at his colleagues. In a deliberate hash of English, Vulcan, Old High Martian, medical Latin and Greek, and Fortran—the language used to program very simple-minded computers—he said, "Maab still claims he would have let us go if it hadn't been for my laying hands on that poor girl. But now, apparently, we're sunk. Why do you suppose Scotty hasn't sent down a landing party?"

"By my calculation," Spock said, "it is an hour past the longest time Mr. Scott would wait before taking action. No other conclusion is possible but that he has become engaged in some other duty which he considers more important, as Maab hinted."

Since the First Officer, picking up McCoy's clue, put out several words of this speech in the operative terms of the calculus of statement, he had to repeat it with these parts translated into Vegan before Kirk or McCoy could be sure of it; but once understood, there was no arguing it.

Kirk eyed everyone in the room with slow calculation. Then he said, slowly and in Cerean, "Bones—I think you ought to do what you started out to do before. That girl's burned arm is still untended."

The guards stiffened.

"Might as well," McCoy said, also in Cerean. "They can only kill me once for touching her, after all."

"Mr. Spock, what is your advice?"

"I believe, Captain, that the risk is defensible."

Good; they understood each other. McCoy stood up. As his shadow fell across the girl, she looked up, and then pulled herself together. McCoy kneeled beside her.

"Your arm," he said, very gently.

"You will not touch me!"

The guards took a step forward. McCoy reached out. Eleen promptly turned into a scratching, biting wildcat.

Somehow or other, it had occurred to none of them, in their swift and necessarily cryptic plotting, that she would also squeal. McCoy clamped a hand down hard over her mouth.

It was this, evidently, that made up the guards' minds. They lunged away from the entrance toward the struggle. Their backs were toward Kirk and Spock for perhaps three seconds. No more than three seconds later, they were decked.

While Spock disarmed the unconscious men, Kirk leaned over the girl, whom McCoy was still holding silent with grim difficulty.

"Listen, Eleen," Kirk said. "We're leaving. We can leave you behind, if that's what you want. Or you can cooperate and come with us. Maybe, just maybe, we can get you safely to our ship. We offer you the choice. Will you come with us?"

Cautiously, McCoy removed his hand from her mouth, ready to clamp it back down at the slightest intake of breath for a scream. But the girl only glared. At last she said, "I am dishonored. But I wish to live. I will come."

McCoy helped her up by the uninjured arm. She pulled away from him and stood immobile, not deigning to speak further, and waited while Spock distributed the guards' weapons to Kirk and McCoy, retaining a *klugat* for himself.

"Now," Kirk said, "let's get those phasers and communicators back."

This was not as easy in the doing as in the saying. Outside, the tribesmen were seated around the rebuilt campfire in an open square, the open end of which was occupied solely by Maab, with Keel standing in the background. Kirk and Spock approached the back of Akaar's tent stealthily, slit the fabric, and slipped inside.

While they searched, they heard Maab's voice: ". . . Only the woman lives now. All know her. And it is not only the child that dooms her."

A general rumble of agreement.

Kirk threw back a carpet over a chest. There were the belts with the communicators still on them, but the phasers were gone. Somebody in this crowd, then, knew which was which—another oddity. He and Spock had just begun to look further when there was a mutter of movement and conversation outside, and a second later McCoy's head popped through the slit in the tent fabric.

"Jim," he whispered urgently. "The Council meeting's over. They're going to find out we're gone . . ."

As if in confirmation, there was a shout of alarm in the near distance.

The three men and Eleen stumbled through the scrub until the light from the fire and the torches was the dimmest possible glow in the distance before Kirk chanced calling a halt. Kneeling and motioning the others to cover —what there was of it in this brush—he snapped open his communicator. "Kirk to *Enterprise* . . . Kirk to *Enterprise* . . . Come in, Scotty . . . Kirk to *Enterprise* . . ."

There was no answer. Had the device been sabotaged? Kirk held out his hand for Spock's communicator, but that produced no better results.

"They are operative," said the First Officer. "It would appear that the *Enterprise* is simply out of range."

"Out of range?" McCoy said. "Where would they go?"

"The answer to that would involve a great deal of useless speculation on our part, Doctor, since we have no facts at hand. A better question is, what do we do until the ship returns?"

"No place can hide you from the *makeen*," the woman said abruptly.

"What are they?" Kirk said. "Or it?"

"There are legends," Spock said, "of a guild of assassins among the Cerean tribes—a secret society, outside the law."

"They are not outside the law," Eleen said. "They are a part of our society. Certain deaths are always— necessary."

"Criminals like us?" Kirk said. "And 'traitors' like your husband? And you?"

"*Not* me," Eleen said. Her voice was angry, harsh, bitter. "It is because I bear Akaar's child. I did not want it. I would kill it myself, if that would save me."

McCoy took her by the wrist, and his own voice was just as angry. "You listen to me, Missy. You're not killing

93

anything while I'm here to prevent it. We intend to keep both you *and* your baby alive, whether you want it or not. Hear me?"

She twisted herself free, her face contorted with anger and loathing. "You are heard. And I come with you because you will give me a few more hours to live. But in the end you will not escape the *makeen*."

"Maybe not," Kirk said. "But we sure in blazes are going to try."

By the first wash of daybreak there were ample signs that they were being followed. Kirk was almost sorry to see the intimations of dawn, for at night he had at least been able to guess how far ahead they were of their pursuers by the distant sparks of torches.

The light found them in rocky country, the foothills of a mountain range. It was chill and desolate, even in the pale gold of early sunlight. The trail they were following seemed to wander aimlessly; Kirk could only hope that this was because it was following the contours of the land, rather than being simply an animal trail.

He and Spock led the way, with Eleen close behind. As bulky as her physical condition made her, she was surprisingly fresh and strong; McCoy, puffing along behind her, looked more the worse for wear than she did.

But the day grew hotter, the slopes steeper, the footing strewn with slippery shale and broken rock. At last Eleen stumbled and would have fallen had McCoy not caught her. She still had the energy to break free of him, however.

"Stay here with her and let her rest, Bones," Kirk said. "We're going to look around. While you're waiting, treat that arm—by force, if necessary."

He moved off with Spock. Shortly, they found the trail entering the narrow mouth of a steep defile. The slopes were shale-strewn and very high.

"Nice place to get trapped in," Kirk said.

"It has advantages as well, Captain. A defensible entrance, and walls that provide difficult access for attackers."

"That may be. At least there also seems to be a way

out. If we could block this entrance, that would hold them up; they'd have to go around, over the hills."

Spock's eyebrows went up. He looked about speculatively. "The entrance is narrow enough, and there seems to be enough loose rock."

"What do you have in mind?"

"Do you remember our discussion of the kinds of weapons that might be made with a communicator in an emergency? In this instance, I think the device I called a 'sound bomb' might be in order." Kirk promptly handed Spock his communicator, but the First Officer shook his head. "Captain, it's only a chance. I would have to phase *two* communicator signals into exact synchronization. We only have three. The odds . . ."

"I'm not interested in the exact odds—only in lowering them. I'll go get McCoy's communicator."

He went back. He found Eleen's arm bandaged. He shook hands with himself at McCoy with approval, but McCoy was frowning.

"Jim, she says the baby isn't due until next week, but as far as I can tell with the few instruments I have, it's due *now*."

"Oh, brrrotherrr. Well, you've doubtless delivered plenty of babies."

"Sure. But the Cereans have been away from Earth a long time, and they've developed some differences from the basic humanoid stock—a process called 'genetic drift' that's common in small, inbred populations. And if surgical intervention's necessary . . ."

"We may not live long enough to worry about it. Give me your communicator, Bones, and come along. We're planning a surprise."

Spock worked quickly, explaining to McCoy as he went along. "I have placed these so the sound beams they put out will meet and focus on a weak point, a potential slide area. The phased beams should set up a vibration in the rocks, *beneath* the loose material. There the rock is cohesive enough so that the vibration should build to the equivalent of explosive force."

"And the whole thing," Kirk said, "will end up in Maab's lap. We hope."

"Theoretically, if the loose rock does not slide away too soon and allow the sound energy to escape as heat. In either event it will destroy the communicators."

Kirk glanced back. Tiny figures were on the horizon. Their pace obviously had picked up. These tribesmen were like bloodhounds, and the track was fresh.

"Let's go." Kirk and Spock twisted the dials of the two communicators. The dull black little instruments each began to emit a hum which rose quickly in pitch to an earsplitting screech. Hastily, the party ran up the trail into the defile.

A glance back showed that their harriers were also running. The sound had located their quarry for them.

The rising sounds merged into one intolerable note. Eleen clutched at her head, then at her belly. McCoy grabbed her around the waist, kept her moving.

The screaming note was joined by a groaning rumble of rock shaking free of its moorings. Suddenly, the screaming wail was gone, leaving a silence which only seemed underlined by the moan of protesting rock.

Then came the explosion, the confined energy bursting out of the cliffside as though an actual charge had been planted there. The rocks crumbled and fell apart, their grumbling rising to a thunder as the shale and dirt smashed down the slope.

Maab, Keel and their party were almost in the defile. They looked up as the rock slide bore down on them. After a split second of frozen terror, they wheeled and scattered like a flight of pigeons. But some of them were caught, all the same.

And in the end, the entrance to the defile was gone. Instead, there was only a massive heap of shale, boulders and dirt.

"Very nice, Mr. Spock," Kirk said, when he could hear again. "Now, we'd better push on. There's still the problem of food and water . . . "

"Not a chance, Jim," McCoy said. "We might carry Eleen—but not very far. She's started labor."

Since they had no choice, they did carry her out the other end of the defile; they did not want the *makeens* to return the favor by dropping rocks on them from above. At the exit, the country opened out a little, and off to the right some green shrub growth and contorted young trees indicated the possible presence of water.

Kirk looked up the slopes. A peculiar formation caught his eye: several huge boulders tumbled together, with a narrow, dark opening just visible between them. Kirk pointed.

"We might take shelter under those rocks. It's probably the best we can do on such short notice. Spock, stay here while we take her up and stand guard."

The First Officer nodded, and unhooking the *klugat* he had taken from the guard, twirled it experimentally.

The hole proved to be a genuine cave. The entrance was low, but inside the roof was high enough to permit them to stand erect. It was far from spacious, however. The walls were rough and pitted, and the floor sloped. Eleen lowered her bulky body and sat huddled in pain.

"Even eighteenth-century surgeons had more to work with than this," McCoy said, "but I guess beggars can't be choosers."

"We'll be outside if you need help."

"Don't make any rash offers."

Kirk went outside to find Spock experimenting with the *klugat*. "A most unusual weapon," the First Officer said. "Observe that the cutting edge is along the *inside*. If you throw it with a snap of the wrist, thus . . ."

The whirling knife spun in flight, its silver blades flashing. It sliced into a low bush and nearly cut it free of the ground before becoming entangled.

"And if you miss, it comes back to the owner," Spock said, retrieving the weapon. "A nice instance of economy."

"We'll need the economy. We've only got two. I'm more interested in those saplings. They look resilient. We might make bows and arrows—if we only had something to use for bowstrings."

"Hmm," Spock said. "A very pretty problem. I see nothing that would serve. But Captain, I suggest that an even more primitive weapon might serve our purposes: a throwing-stick."

"What in blazes is that?"

"It consists of a grooved handle with a cupped end. The arrow is fitted into the groove with the arrowhead toward the hand and the feathered end in the cup. You swing the throwing-stick overhand, and the arrow leaves it with considerable force, on the lever principle."

"There's plenty of flint here for arrowheads," Kirk said thoughtfully. "But we have nothing to use for feathers."

"True. However, if we notch the end of the arrow and tie on a length of rag, that may afford some stabilization, on the principle of a kite's tail. And may I point out, Captain, that the only missile weapon possessed by the Cereans is this *klugat*, which has a range limit built into it by the very fact that it is designed to return to the thrower. Our arrows will fly somewhat farther—and will, of course, be quite unfamiliar to the Cereans. These advantages are small, but they may be all we have."

"You're right, Mr. Spock. Let's get to work."

As they climbed toward the cave, a cry of pain came from it.

They were practicing with the throwing-sticks when McCoy at last appeared at the cave entrance, mopping his hands. "Come on in," he said.

Eleen lay in a shadowed corner. Her light cloak was her only bed; the lower half of her long tunic had been torn off to provide a blanket for the small bundle lying beside her. She propped herself up as the men entered, but made no protest as Kirk and Spock peered down at the bundle.

Tiny fists that resembled minute starfish wriggled aimlessly. The baby yawned into Kirk's face, seeming to suggest that the whole thing had been a snap, and all McCoy's worries had been needless.

"It seems a rather average specimen on the whole," Spock said.

"You think so, Spock?" McCoy said tiredly. "Well, look again. That is the High Chief of the ten tribes of Ceres."

He picked up the baby and put it in its mother's arms. The woman took it, passively, but she said, "I do not want it."

"He's your son," Kirk said.

"I did not wish it. It was good to become wife to

98

Akaar. He was High Chief and had wealth. I thought because he was old and already had a son . . ."

"I don't care why you married Teer Akaar," Kirk interrupted harshly. "You did, and you bore his son, who is now the High Chief. You're bound by honor and position to care for him as long as you live. That's your tradition as well as ours, and I'll enforce it if I have to. Bones, how soon can she travel?"

"All these Cereans seem to have remarkable stamina, and I'd say this one is strong as an ox, even now. We might be able to move as soon as tomorrow."

"If so," Spock said, "I suggest that we climb the ridge behind us when we leave, and move cross-country. It will be difficult, but I believe safer."

Kirk thought about this. Maab might well have figured that they would follow the defile all the way, because of the woman. Or he might even already be moving in on them from the other end.

"Even odds," he said "We'll try it. But first, let's get some sleep. McCoy, you need the rest most; you'll stand last guard. I'll take the first."

He awoke to hear McCoy's voice calling his name and feeling his shoulder being shaken. As he sat up, McCoy was already leaving his side to rouse the sleeping Spock.

"Wake up, Spock. Jim, we're in more trouble. My, uh, patient has taken the child and gone."

"She got past *you?*" Kirk said.

"She struck me from behind with a rock. We've got to have more respect for the medical profession around here."

"How long has she been gone?"

"By the sun, I was out no more than half an hour. Her trail leads toward the defile exit. If Maab's men catch her . . ."

"I suggest," Spock said, "that henceforth we leave the matter to tribal justice, and devote ourselves to our own survival."

"Why, you ice-hearted, unfeeling . . ."

"The lady is *not* honorable, or charitable, or cooperative, or of much total worth," Spock said. "Even you can see that, Doctor."

"Yes? And what about the baby?"

"You both have a point," Kirk said. "Granted that the lady has few shining virtues. But the baby has done nothing but come into this world. I'd like to see him get a chance to grow up in it. Let's get going."

They moved cautiously along the defile, keeping as high up on the slopes as the footing would allow. At the exit, they came upon an astonishing scene.

The assassins, or all that had survived the rock slide, were all there, and so was Eleen. Most of the men were staring at her in amazement, and small wonder, for she was holding out the child to Maab.

"I have the child, Maab," she said, her voice distant but clear. "He is yours. Do as you will."

Keel and Maab looked at each other. At last Maab said, "Why?"

"I claim nothing but my life. Take the child, Maab—but let me go free. I care not for *him*."

Finally Maab nodded. When he spoke, his voice was sarcastic. "It is much like you, Eleen. Come with us."

At this point, Kirk rose from cover and swung the throwing-stick, then fell flat again in the brush. No one saw him. The arrow cut through the air straight at Maab, its rag tail fluttering, and at the last minute veering and hitting another man in the leg. Evidently feathers were much better for arrows than tails were. The struck man fell, with a cry as much of surprise as of pain.

Everyone turned toward him. Spock popped up from behind a rock and threw, then also vanished. The arrow winged Keel; a red stain began to spread on his sleeve.

McCoy now appeared suddenly on the trail, just behind Eleen. Grabbing her from behind, he dragged her screaming to cover. The assassins were now beginning to realize what had happened, and made an abortive move after McCoy, but a scatter of arrows from Kirk and Spock threw them into confusion. The volume of fire was, tactically, not nearly great enough to produce such an effect; evidently Spock's guess about the effect on morale of the unfamiliarity of the weapons had been correct.

"Bones, get out of there!" Kirk shouted. "General retreat!"

He ducked as Keel threw a *klugat* at him. The vicious scything blades slashed the air whisperingly over his head. Below, McCoy, dragging Eleen, made his way up the slope from cover to cover. Kirk slipped to another rock, rose, and threw again, and this time was rewarded with a full-throated scream. He was getting the hang of the thing.

They moved backward slowly, covering for Eleen, hampered by the baby. As they went, Spock picked up the *klugat* Keel had thrown, which had been blocked from boomeranging by a boulder. Oddly, the *makeen* were no longer following.

Back inside the more defensible defile walls, the *Enterprise* men paused to assess the situation. They were nicely trapped—and the arrows were running out.

"What did you think you were going to do?" McCoy said, glaring at Eleen.

"You heard," she said coldly. "I would trade my life. Maab will let me go—to get the child."

"Oh? Aren't you overlooking something? We were close enough behind you to surprise Maab. It might even have looked to him like you were bait for a trap. He won't trust you again, Missy—if he ever did. He'll kill you both, just to be sure."

"And of what use was this grand surprise?" the woman said with contempt. "Here he can simply starve us out."

As Kirk digested the truth of that, Maab's voice rang out.

"Captain!"

"What is it?"

Maab came forward, slowly, accompanied by two henchmen. The other assassins followed, stopping just out of arrow range. They learn fast, Kirk thought ruefully.

"A fine fight, Captain. And fought with much ingenuity. But useless, as you can see. I suggest that you put down your weapons now."

Clearly, there was no choice. "Do as he says, Doctor, Mr. Spock," Kirk said quietly. "It appears that the cavalry doesn't come over the hill any more."

Eleen pushed forward, the child held out in her arms. "Take him, Maab. He is all that prevents your true Chieftanship."

Maab signaled to a henchman, who came forward and took the child.

"I will go now," Eleen said, hopefully.

"No," Maab said. "You stand condemned for other treasons. You know the penalty for unfaithfulness."

The woman backed away in terror. "No, no! I was not unfaithful—there was no one . . ."

"There is proof," Maab said heavily. "Keel saw it done, though he did not name the man before he was slain by this alien Captain's arrow. My brother may be dead, but his honor is my honor. Let justice be done!"

"No! No!"

Eleen began to run. The *makeen* silently cleared for her what seemed to be an avenue of escape. Then a *klugat* whirled through the air. She fell, and was still.

Maab looked sharply at Kirk. "You do not protest as before."

"Your justice is served," Kirk said, fighting down his nausea. "Perhaps it was merited. But the child is a different matter. He has harmed no one."

"He lives. The High Chieftanship must be mine."

"Why? Clearly you have only sown the seeds of still more factionalism, still more assassination. What do you really gain in the end, Maab? And who else gains with you?"

"You are a clever man, Captain," Maab said reflectively. "You see beneath surfaces. Well, you are not the only ones who wish this rock in our hills. The Klingon Empire offered my brother much for mining rights. Wealth, power, a seat in their Empire. The fool chose to honor a promise made to your Federation. He did not trust the Klingons."

"But you did."

"I had to be Chief to give them what they wanted. A Klingon ship drew yours away so your men could not stop Akaar's death. You could have returned without harm if you had not broken taboo to save Eleen. She was not worth your deaths."

"She was," McCoy said, "then."

"Because of the child within her? But both die in the end. All this that followed was fruitless."

102

"One thing, then," McCoy said. "Let me have the boy I brought into the world. If you're going to take us out of it, I'd rather have him with me."

Maab shrugged and signaled to his henchman, who paused and then passed the child to McCoy. The remaining assassins raised their *klugats*. The resemblance to a firing squad was inarguable . . .

*"Drop those weapons!"*

The voice—Scott's voice—came from the lip of the cliff. With him was Sulu and a crewman. At the edge of the other side of the defile were Frost and two more crewmen—all with phasers at the ready.

"What the devil?" McCoy said.

"I would say, Doctor," Spock said, "that the cavalry has just come over the hill."

The crewmen came down, herding the assassins together. "But *how*?" Maab said. "How did you escape the Klingon ship? They were not to let you through until I signaled . . ."

"They backed off and ran when we came straight at them," Sulu said with a grin. "At first they decoyed us away with false distress calls, but when we saw through that and went right down their throats—well, their ships have speed, I'll grant them that."

Scott added, "I didn't think the Klingons were ready for a war, even to please this gentleman. Not even for topaline mining rights."

"Mr. Scott," Kirk said, "I know you for a resourceful man, but how did you find us out here?"

"When we beamed down to the main camp, we found what had happened. A lot of Akaar's followers are left; only the assassins of Maab's group went hunting you. They told us you'd escaped to the hills, we used our sensors to pinpoint you, and beamed down again. 'Twas a near squeak."

Abruptly, there was movement behind Maab and a knife flashed. Maab gasped and fell. His killer stolidly wiped the knife on the sleeve of his tunic and held it out to a stunned Kirk.

"For treason to Akaar," the man said, "and for treason with the Klingons. I now stand ready for justice."

"And who in blazes may you be?" Kirk demanded.

"I," the man said, "am the father of the High Chief born of Eleen."

The treaty was signed, by the father, who after a long tribal parley had been named the High Chief's guardian-regent. What complicated tribal politics and concepts of justice produced this result, Kirk could not fathom, nor did he care any longer. It was enough for him that the man had bound himself to serve the child until it came of age.

The last surprise was the naming of the High Chief. The father dubbed him, Leonard James Akaar.

It was Spock's opinion that McCoy and the Captain were going to be insufferably pleased with themselves about that for at least a month.

# AMOK TIME*

## (Theodore Sturgeon)

It was actually Nurse Christine Chapel who first noticed that there seemed to be something wrong with Spock. Nothing serious—only that he wasn't eating. McCoy, observing him more closely, saw no further sign but what seemed to be a gradual increase in tension, something that might almost have been called "nervousness" if Spock hadn't been half Vulcan. This, McCoy thought, might have been purely a subjective impression on his own part.

It wasn't. On the third day of the apparent fast, Nurse Chapel tried to tempt the First Officer with a vile green concoction called plomik soup, regarded as a delicacy on Vulcan. Spock threw the bowl at her, soup and all.

This was enough to move McCoy to suggest to Spock, a day after the soup incident and apparently without any connection to it, that it was time for his routine checkup.

The logical, unemotional First Officer's verbatim reply to this was, "You will cease to pry into my personal affairs, Doctor, or I shall certainly break your neck."

Regardless of his state of mind—whatever it was— Spock certainly knew that this would not go unreported. He forestalled inquiry by requesting a leave of absence on his home planet. On the present course of the *Enterprise,* he pointed out, a diversion to Vulcan would cost a loss of only 2.8 light-days.

Unfortunately, Kirk had to refuse him. In all the years

*Hugo Award nominee

that Kirk had known him, Spock had never asked for a leave of any sort, and in fact had refused offers; he had leave enough accumulated for six men. But the *Enterprise* was bound for the inauguration ceremonies of the new president of Altair Six—not, apparently, a vital assignment, but the orders left no leeway for side trips, all the same. Kirk suggested that shore leave facilities on Altair Six were excellent; Spock declined the offer stiffly, and that was that.

At least, that should have been that. Not six hours later, while the First Officer was off duty, Kirk discovered that the ship's course had been altered for Vulcan anyhow, on Spock's orders. Leaving the bridge in Scott's charge, Kirk went directly down to Spock's quarters.

He had seldom visited them before, but he resisted the impulse to look around. He got only the vague impression of a room simple, sparse and vaguely Oriental in decoration and mood, the quarters of a warrior in the field. Spock was seated at a desk studying a small reading screen. Kirk had the briefest of impressions that the screen showed the head of a very young girl, no more than a child, but Spock snapped it off too quickly for him to be sure.

"Well, Mr. Spock?"

"Well, Captain?"

"I want an explanation. Why did you change our course?"

"Sir?"

"You changed our course for Vulcan. I want to know why."

Spock frowned slightly. "I changed our course?"

"You deny it?"

"No," Spock said. "By no means, Captain. It is—quite possible."

"Then why did you do it?"

"Captain," Spock said, "I accept, on your word, that I did it. But I do not know why. Nor do I remember doing it." He looked straight at Kirk, his spine stiffening. "And therefore I request that you put me in confinement—securely—where I can neither see nor be seen by any. one."

"But why?"

"Captain, lock me away. I do not wish to be seen. I cannot . . . No Vulcan could explain further."

"Spock, I'm trying to help you . . ."

"Ask me no further questions!" Spock almost shouted. "I will not answer!"

"All right," Kirk said evenly. "I'll accede to your request. But first, I order you to report to Sickbay, Mr. Spock. McCoy's waiting."

"I don't know how Spock exists with his kind of internal setup," McCoy said. "His normal pulse is in the 240 beats-per-minute range, his blood pressure almost nonexistent by our standards—not that I consider that green stuff of his to be entirely comparable to blood. But that's only Spock under normal conditions, Jim. As matters stand now, if we don't get him to Vulcan within eight days—or maybe only seven—he'll die."

"*Die?* But why? What's the matter with him?"

"I don't know," McCoy said. "All I can tell you is that there's a growing imbalance of bodily functions. As if in your or my bodies, huge amounts of adrenalin were constantly being secreted into our bloodstreams. Spock won't say why. But unless it's stopped somehow, the physical and emotional pressures will kill him."

"You're convinced he knows what it is?"

"Yes. But he won't tell me."

"He's in the solitary confinement he asked for now?"

"Yes, Jim. And—I wouldn't approach him, if I were you. It's a shocking thing to have to say, but—well, I consider him irrational."

"I'll see him anyhow. What else can I do? There's *got* to be an answer."

"I suppose so," McCoy said. "But Jim—watch out."

"Mr. Spock," Kirk said, as gently as possible. "McCoy gave me his evaluation of your condition."

Spock remained silent, his face averted.

"Spock, he says you'll die unless something is done. *What?* Is it something only your planet can do for you?"

No answer.

"Mr. Spock. You have been called the best First Officer in the Fleet. That is an enormous asset to me. If I have to lose that First Officer, I want to know why."

Spock stirred, and then began to speak in an almost inaudible voice. "It is a thing that no . . . outworlder may know—except for the very few that have been involved. A Vulcan understands—but even we do not speak of it among ourselves. It is a deeply personal thing. Captain, cannot you let it rest at that?"

"I cannot," Kirk said. "My ship, my command, my duty are all at stake. I require you to explain. If I must, I'll order you to explain."

"Captain—some things transcend even the discipline of the service."

"That may sometimes be true. But nothing transcends the health, safety and well-being of the members of my crew. Would it help to promise you that I'd consider anything you say to me to be totally confidential?"

Spock hesitated a long moment. At last he said, "It has to do with—with . . ."

The last word was quite inaudible. Kirk said, "With what?"

"Biology."

"What kind of biology?"

"Vulcan biology."

"You mean, the biology *of* Vulcans? Biology, as in reproduction? Oh, blazes! That's nothing to be embarrassed about. It even happens to birds and bees."

Spock stared at the floor. "The birds and bees are not Vulcans. If they were—if any creature were as proudly logical as we—and had their logic ripped from them—as this time does to us . . ."

Kirk waited.

"How do Vulcans find their mates?" Spock said. "Haven't you wondered, Captain? How are we selected, one for the other? I'm sure you've heard many jokes on the subject. We are so aloof, so proud, so without feeling, that we invite such jokes."

"Yes, I've heard them," Kirk said. "But jokes aside, I guess the rest of us assume, well, that it's done, uh, quite logically. Eugenically, perhaps."

"It—is not. We shield it with ritual and custom, as shrouded in antiquity as our seven moons. You humans have no conception—it strips our minds from us. It brings a—a madness which rips away our veneer of civilization." Spock slumped, his face pinched with agony. "It is the *pon farr*—the time of mating."

"But you're not a salmon or an eel, man! You're . . ."

"Half human," Spock finished, painfully. "I had hoped that that would spare me this. But my Vulcan blood is too strong. It drives me home, to take a wife in Vulcan fashion. Or else, as Dr. McCoy says, to die."

"Dear God," Kirk said. The lumps in his own belly and throat were now almost too great for him to bear. He could only vaguely imagine what it had cost Spock to tell him this much.

Was there any way out? There were three starships expected to attend the inauguration ceremony: the *Enterprise,* the *Excalibur* and the *Endeavour.* Neither of the others was within range to get Spock to Vulcan in time.

It was not that vital to have three starships at the ceremony, but the orders specified it. If Kirk disobeyed, Starship Command would . . .

Never mind. Kirk owed his life to Spock, not just once, but half a dozen times. That was worth a career. Kirk stepped to the intercom.

"Mr. Chekov, Kirk here. Maintain course for Vulcan. Warp Eight."

"Uh—yes, sir," Chekov's startled voice said.

"Kirk out."

"Captain," Spock said in a low voice.

"Yes, Mr. Spock."

"Something happens to us at this time, almost—an insanity—an insanity you—no doubt would find distasteful."

"Should I? You've been patient with my kinds of madness."

"Then—will you beam down with me to the surface of Vulcan, and stand with me? There is a brief ceremony. By tradition, the male is attended by his closest friends."

"Thank you, Mr. Spock."

"Also—I believe Doctor McCoy has also guessed the

reason behind all this, and has kept his own counsel, and my secret. I would like him to accompany us."

"I believe," Kirk said slowly, "that he will be honored."

The three beamed down to a fairly level arena area. Rocks around its edges gave it a half-natural, half-artificial aspect, as if the wind and rain had carved something like a Stonehenge, or reduced a Stonehenge to something like this. Inside it, there was an open temple—two high arches of stone, an open fire pit, several huge, jade-like wind chimes stirring and chiming in the hot breeze. The rest of the landscape was drifting sand, stretching away to a distant saw-toothed line of mountains jutting up at the edge of the far horizon.

"The land of my family," Spock said. "Our place for mating. It has been held by us for more than two thousand Earth years!" He choked, and gestured toward the temple. "This—is *Koon-ut-Kal-if-fee*. It means, 'The place of marriage and challenge.' In the distant past, we—killed to win our mates. It is still a time of dread for us. Perhaps, the price we pay—for no emotion the rest of the time."

"If it's any of my business—" McCoy began.

"You were invited, Doctor."

"Then—you said this T'Pring you are to meet was already your wife."

"By our parents' arrangement. A ceremony, while we were but seven years of age. One touches the other—thus —as you have seen me do to feel another's thoughts. In this way, our minds were locked together—so that at the proper time we would both be drawn to *Koon-ut-Kal-if-fee.*"

There sounded a distant bell, harmonizing well with the heavier notes of the wind chimes, and then figures began to appear among the rocks. There seemed to be eight or ten of them. Heading the procession, four Vulcan men were carrying someone in an ornate litter or sedan chair. Two other members of the party carried bright-colored, ceremonial objects which consisted of dozens of tiny bells attached to an ornate frame on a pole.

As they drew closer, Kirk saw that the person inside the

litter was an old woman of immensely authoritative bearing; as the litter was set down and she emerged from it, he recognized her with a shock as one of the high Vulcan elders, T'Pau, the only person who had ever turned down a seat on the Federation Council. Characteristically, Spock had never mentioned that his family was this important.

The bride walked beside her, no child now, but a lithe, graceful, beautiful woman, even by Earth standards. Behind her strode a tall, muscular and rather handsome Vulcan male; and behind him, a slightly shorter but even stronger-looking man who carried a Vulcan war ax. The rest of the procession moved in stately grace behind these principals.

Spock turned and walked to one of the huge wind chimes. Picking up a stone mallet, he struck the chimes, producing a somber male sound which was answered by the shaking of the bell banners. T'Pring seated herself on a carved rock at the temple archway. T'Pau stood in the open in front of the temple, with her back to it and the girl. The muscular young Vulcan stood next to the arch, like a big brick gatepost, while the rest of the entourage lined up in a curve behind them.

With a sudden swift movement, T'Pau raised both her arms. Spock stepped forward and bowed before her. She laid both her hands on his shoulders, as if in a blessing, and then looked beyond him to Kirk and McCoy.

"Spock. Are our ceremonies for outworlders?"

"They are not outworlders," Spock said. "They are my friends. I am permitted this. Their names are Kirk and McCoy. I pledge their behavior with my life."

"Very well." T'Pau turned to the bearers of the bell banners. "*Kah-if-fee!*"

The bell banners were shaken. Spock turned to strike the wind chimes again with his stone mallet—but at the same instant the girl T'Pring sprang to her feet and cried out:

"*Kah-if-FARR!*"

There was a gasp from the Vulcan onlookers; even T'Pau's eyes flickered in startled surprise. Spock mouthed the word without speaking it, his breathing quickening, his eyes narrowed to slits. T'Pring crossed to him, took the mallet from his hand, and tossed it aside. Her expression was strangely contemptuous.

The Vulcan with the ax stepped forward. He looked both amused and dangerous, like an experienced executioner.

"Hey, what's this?" McCoy said. "If there's going to be hanky-panky . . ."

"All is in order," the old woman said. "She chooses the challenge."

"What?" McCoy pointed at the executioner. "With *him*?"

"No. He acts only if cowardice is seen. T'Pring will now choose her champion. T'Pring: you have chosen. Are you prepared to become the property of the victor? Not merely his wife, but his chattel, with no other rights or status?"

"I am prepared," T'Pring said.

"Then choose."

T'Pring moved regally out into the arena. She stopped by the huge young Vulcan, who straightened proudly, expectantly, but she moved away from him. Then she turned to T'Pau.

"As it was in the dawn of our days," she said, "as it is today, as it will be through all tomorrows, I make my choice." She turned again. "I choose this man."

And she pointed straight at Kirk.

"Now wait a minute—" Kirk said.

At the same moment, the big young Vulcan stepped forward, obviously outraged. "No!" he cried. "I am to be the one! It was agreed! The honor is mine!"

All at once, everyone in the marriage party seemed to be arguing, all in Vulcan. Under cover of the noise, Kirk said swiftly to McCoy, "What happens if I decline?"

"I don't know, Jim. He'd probably have to fight the young man. And in his present condition, he couldn't win. But Jim, this looks like a situation of total combat—and the heat and the air here are pretty fierce. I'm not sure you could win either—even if you'd want to."

"I'm not about to take a dead First Officer back with me. On the other hand, there's T'Pau over there—all of

Vulcan wrapped up in one package. How will it look if a Starship Captain backs off from this, afraid?"

"But . . ."

"And if I can't beat him, if I'm in any danger, I'll give up. Spock wins, honor is satisfied. Or maybe just knock him out . . ."

*"Kroykah!"* T'Pau said explosively. The hubbub stopped as if turned off by a switch.

The big young Vulcan said, "I ask forgiveness." He went back to his post by the arch, sulky, unrepentant, but no longer defiant.

Kirk said, "I accept." He threw a look toward his First Officer, but Spock seemed oblivious of everything but the ceremony.

"According to our laws," T'Pau said, "combat begins with the *lirpa.*"

Two Vulcan males stepped forward, each carrying a vicious-looking weapon. At one end of a heavy handle was a circular, razor-edged knife; at the other end, a metal cudgel.

"If both survive the *lirpa,*" T'Pau continued, "then combat continues with *ahn woon,* until death. *Klee-et!"*

At this command, Spock wheeled to face Kirk. His eyes blazed with blind savagery as he lifted the weapon. McCoy stepped forward.

"Nothing doing!" McCoy said. "No one mentioned a fight to the death—" his words trailed off as the executioner-like Vulcan stepped in, lifting his ax. Then he swallowed and charged on. "T'Pau, these men are friends. To force them to fight until one is killed . . ."

"Challenge was lawfully given and accepted. Neither party was forced. However, Spock may release the challenger. Spock! How do you choose?"

Spock continued to eye Kirk, scowling. There was still no sign of recognition. Then, suddenly, he shouted his answer, hoarsely, scornfully: *"Klee-fah!"*

"That's it, Bones," Kirk said. "Get out of the combat area. There's nothing you can do."

McCoy stood fast. "I claim one right for him then. Your temperature is hot for our kind, your air is thin . . ."

He was interrupted by a feint from Spock. Kirk

dodged, but Spock, slashing again with the blade, abruptly reversed the weapon and caught Kirk a glancing blow with the cudgel end. Kirk went down, rolling barely in time as Spock reversed again and slashed down hard. The weapon bit into the earth.

Kirk kicked hard at Spock's legs. Now the Vulcan was down, and Kirk was rolling to his feet. He was already sweating, and his breath was whistling in his throat. Out of the corner of his eye, he saw the burly axman advancing on McCoy.

"I can't watch you both, Bones!" he shouted. "Get out before you kill me!"

McCoy held his ground. Turning back toward T'Pau, he produced a hypo from his medical kit. "Are Vulcans afraid of fair combat?" he demanded.

"What is this?"

"A high-G vitalizer shot. To compensate for temperature and atmosphere."

*"Kroykah!"* T'Pau said. Everyone froze. "Very well. Your request is reasonable."

McCoy pressed the hypo against Kirk's arm. It hissed, and the physician turned away.

Spock moved in at once. This time it was Kirk who feinted. Spock countered as if they were marionettes tied to the same string. Kirk tried again, with the same result.

With a wordless rumble, Spock launched a lightning kick at Kirk's left hand. Kirk bent aside, and catching the heel of Spock's boot, dumped him. He dived after him, but Spock rolled with unbelievable quickness, so that Kirk hit only the bare ground.

Then both were up, crouching. Spock raised his weapon as if to throw it, and Kirk tensed, ready to jump aside. Spock, however, suddenly reversed the weapon and rushed.

They came together like the impact of two machines, belly to belly, free hand holding weapon wrist, glaring into each other's eyes. Then, with a bone-cracking wrench, Spock whipped Kirk's weapon to the ground.

With two quick, stamping steps, like a flamenco dancer, Spock snapped the knife blade with a loud crack, and then kicked the cudgel end away. He raised his own blade to striking position.

"Spock!" McCoy cried out. "No!"

They were still at close quarters. Kirk hit Spock's wrist with a karate chop. Now it was Spock's *lirpa* that went flying out of reach.

"*Kroykah!*" T'Pau cried.

Again, Spock froze. The Vulcan weapons attendant came hurrying out, carrying what seemed to be no more than two leather bands about three feet long and four inches wide. One was handed to Spock, who backed up, waiting; Kirk got the other.

"A strip of leather?" Kirk said. "Is that all?"

"The *ahn woon*," T'Pau said. "Oldest and deadliest of Vulcan weapons."

Kirk inspected it with puzzlement. How on earth was one supposed to use this thing? It wasn't long enough to be an effective whip, and . . .

Spock did not hesitate. Scooping up a jagged rock, in the same movement he converted the leather strap into a sling. Kirk understood too late. The rock caught him hard in the ribs, and he fell.

As he staggered to his feet, Spock charged him, now holding one end of the strap in each hand. Whipping it around Kirk's legs, he yanked, and down Kirk went again.

Instantly, Spock was at his back, garroting him with the strap. Kirk shifted to try to throw the First Officer over his shoulder, but something odd seemed to be happening to his muscles; they responded very slowly, and didn't move in the way his brain told them to go.

The pressure around his neck tightened. He made one last grab for Spock's hands, but never even came close. The universe darkened. Blood roared in his ears. He felt himself fall flat, blind and paralyzed.

"*Kroykah!*" came T'Pau's voice, as if from a great distance.

There was a sound of running footsteps, coming closer. Then came McCoy's voice, charged with bitterness:

"Get your hands off him, Spock. It's finished—he's dead."

It was all most peculiar. Kirk could see nothing, feel

115

nothing, was not even sure he was breathing. He was aware of nothing but the voices, as though he were listening to an exchange over the intercom—or attending a play with his back turned to the stage.

T'PAU: I grieve with you, Doctor.

SPOCK: No! I—no, no . . .

McCOY: McCoy to *Enterprise*.

UHURA: *Enterprise*. Lieutenant Uhura here.

McCOY: Have Transporter Room stand by for landing party to beam up. Strange as it may seem, Mr. Spock, you're in command now. Any orders?

SPOCK: I'll—I'll follow you in a few minutes. Instruct Mr. Chekov to plot a course for the nearest base where I must—surrender myself to the authorities . . . T'-Pring.

T'PRING: Yes.

SPOCK: Explain.

T'PRING: Specify.

SPOCK: Why the challenge; why you chose my Captain as your champion.

T'PRING: Stonn wanted me. I wanted him.

SPOCK: I see no logic in preferring Stonn over me.

T'PRING: He is simple and easily controlled. I calculated the possibilities were these: if your Captain were victor, he would not want me, and so I would have Stonn. If you were victor, you would free me because I dared to challenge, and again I would have Stonn. But if you did not free me it would be the same, for you would be gone again, and I would have your name and your property, and Stonn would still be there.

SPOCK: Flawlessly logical.

T'PRING: I am honored.

SPOCK: Stonn! She is yours. After a time, you may find that *having* is not, after all, so satisfying a thing as *wanting*. It is not logical, but it is often true . . . Spock here. Ready to beam up . . . Live long and prosper, T'Pau.

T'PAU: Live long and prosper, Spock.

SPOCK: I shall do neither. I have killed my Captain —and my friend.

116

Then Kirk's hearing went away too, and for a long time thereafter he knew nothing.

He came gradually back to consciousness in the Sickbay. McCoy was bending over him. Nearby was Spock, his hands over his face. His shoulders were shaking.

Nurse Christine came into his field of view, and turning Spock toward the Captain, gently pulled his hands away from his face. Kirk smiled weakly, and spoke in a faint but cheerful voice.

"Mr. Spock—I never thought I'd see the day . . ."

"Captain!" Spock stared down at him, absolutely dazed with astonishment. Then, obviously realizing what his face and voice were revealing, he looked away.

"Christine," McCoy said, "it might be a good idea for Mr. Spock to get some hot food in him. Why don't you feed him some of that awful plomik soup. Then bring him back here for me to run a physical on him. Go on, Spock. She'll explain it to you."

Christine led the First Officer toward the door. But just before he left, Spock said, "It is not awful plomik soup. It is very good plomik soup."

Then he was gone. Kirk and McCoy smiled after him. Then Kirk rolled his head back and wiped the smile off his face.

"You, Mister," he said, "are a quack."

McCoy shrugged. "I made a mistake. Shot you with ronoxiline D by mistake. Nobody lied. You were dead— by all normal standards. I had to get you back up here fast, or you would have been dead by *any* standards."

"Will Spock be all right?"

"I think so. I'll run a full physical on him to make sure."

Kirk started to sit up. "Where are we now?"

"Stay right there," McCoy said, shoving him back. "We're still orbiting Vulcan."

Kirk reached out and snapped on the bedside intercom. "Kirk to Bridge."

"Bridge, sir. Sulu here."

"Take us out of orbit, Mr. Sulu. Have the navigator lay in a course for Altair Six at top warp speed. Tell Scotty to pour it on—we've got an inauguration to make!"

"Yes *sir*. Bridge out."

As Kirk dropped back onto the bed, McCoy said sourly, "You know, Jim, some one of these days these ceremonies will be the death of you."

"In which case, Bones, remember: you have standing orders to bring me back to life."